ATTENTION

This is an uncorrected proof. It is not a finished book and is not expected to look like one.

Errors in spelling, page length, format, etc., all will be corrected when the book is published several months from now.

Uncorrected proof in this form, might be called pre-publicity proof. It was invented so that you, the reader, might know months before actual publication what the author and publisher are offering.

PEN PALS:
BOOK ONE

BOYS WANTED!

by Sharon Dennis Wyeth

A YEARLING BOOK

Published by
Dell Publishing
a division of
Bantam Doubleday Dell Publishing Group, Inc.
666 Fifth Avenue
New York, New York 10103

Copyright © 1989 by Parachute Press, Inc.

All rights reserved. No part of this book may be reproduced or transmitted in any form or by any means, electronic or mechanical, including photocopying, recording or by any information storage and retrieval system, without the written permission of the Publisher, except where permitted by law.

The trademark Yearling® is registered in the U.S. Patent and Trademark Office.

ISBN: 0-440-40224-7
Published by arrangement with Parachute Press, Inc.
Printed in the United States of America
September 1989
10 9 8 7 6 5 4 3 2 1

For Sims

CHAPTER ONE

"What a bore—having a stupid get-acquainted party on a Saturday night!" Palmer Durand grumbled as she dragged herself into the Fox Hall dormitory. The pretty 13-year-old stopped at the hall mirror and untied her silk neck scarf.

"I thought it was fun," Amy Ho disagreed, squeezing in front of Palmer at the mirror. "It sounds like they have some neat after-school activities here," she said.

The two roommates couldn't have been more different. Palmer (who was born in Palm Beach, Florida) was tall and willowy; while Amy (who was born in Taiwan) was short and athletic-looking. Palmer's blond wavy hair fell to her shoulders, while Amy's jet-black hair was chopped off in a spiked punky style. But it wasn't just a matter of fashion. It sometimes seemed there was nothing they agreed on.

A moment of silence passed before tall, dark-haired Lisa McGreevy chimed in. "You have to admit that the brownies were incredible," she said cheerfully. "I liberated four big ones," she added, pulling the sweets from the pocket of her oversized shirt and laying them out on the hall table.

Shanon Davis gazed at the brownies longingly. "I can't eat those," she sighed, scrunching her face into a sad expression and twisting a strand of her sandy-colored hair. "Chocolate makes me break out."

1

The four freshmen were new to the Alma Stephens School for Girls just outside of Brighton, New Hampshire. Two days ago they'd been strangers, living miles apart. Now they all roomed together in the same suite—Suite 3-D: Palmer and Amy in one bedroom; Lisa and Shanon in the other.

It had been a long day and the girls were tired as they trudged up the wide wooden staircase to their rooms, each lost in her own thoughts.

How am I going to deal with the dress code here? Amy wondered silently. The daughter of a Chinese businessman, Amy Ho had been born in Washington, D.C., but she'd gone to school in more countries and cities than she could count—everywhere from Sydney, Australia, to Bangkok, Thailand. At her most recent school, in New York City, she had practically lived in her black stretch pants, T-shirts, and a beat-up motorcycle jacket. In spring she'd switched to the lightweight black and gold silk jacket that her aunt had brought when she visited from Taiwan two years ago. But those outfits were off limits now. It was strictly dresses, skirts, and blouses at Alma.

Shanon was also thinking about clothes—but for different reasons. To her, all the girls at Alma seemed so beautifully dressed. She'd never been very fashion-conscious before, but now the simple skirts and blouses her mother had made for her seemed dull and old-fashioned. *It doesn't matter,* she told herself brightly. *You're at a great school with nice people. That's all that counts.* She'd known the other girls would be from wealthy families when she accepted the scholarship. Although Shanon had spent her whole life in Brighton, the exclusive Alma Stephens School had always seemed worlds away. Now

2

she was actually a third-former—that's what they called freshmen at Alma—and Shanon could hardly believe her good luck.

Shanon turned and smiled at Lisa, who was walking behind her. "Hey, there," she said, waving a hand in front of Lisa's distant eyes. "You look awfully serious. What were you just thinking about?"

Lisa started, as if her mind had been very far away. "I was trying to figure out what my family would be doing right now," she answered. "I guess I'm a little homesick." Lisa had been dying to come to Alma Stephens. Her mother had gone there, and Lisa grew up hearing wonderful stories about the place. Lisa just hadn't counted on how far away her home in Pennsylvania would seem once she arrived at the school.

"Do you have your keys, Palmer?" Lisa asked when they stopped at the suite door. "I think I left mine inside."

"Of course I do," Palmer said in a slightly superior tone as she fished in her designer purse. *I can see I'm going to have my hands full with these three,* Palmer told herself, unlocking the door. She was not looking forward to communal living at all. It was going to be a big change from the large room with the private bath she was used to at her home in Florida. When her mother enrolled her at Alma, Palmer had consoled herself by thinking that at least she'd be out on her own. But when she heard about Alma's long list of rules and regulations, she decided boarding school was going to be a total drag. There was another thing Palmer disliked about Alma: the scenery. Everywhere she looked she saw the same thing—girls! Even most of the teachers were female.

"Hi," called Maggie Grayson, the French teacher and

3

faculty advisor for Fox Hall. "How was the party? Did you get the list of extracurriculars?"

"The list looks great," Lisa said. "I'm going to check out the art studio and pottery shop."

"I'm interested in the newspaper," Shanon said shyly.

"You'll have to talk to Dolores Countee about that. She's editor-in-chief of *The Ledger*," said Miss Grayson.

"I've seen her around," said Shanon. "She's that tall redhead. I hear she's active in lots of things."

Miss Grayson smiled. "She's a real go-getter, it's true. She always—" With a quick glance at her watch, the young teacher suddenly interrupted herself. "Excuse me," she said. "I really must be going now. I'm expecting a very important call." And she hurried off down the hall.

"At least someone has her own phone," grumbled Palmer, opening the door to Suite 3-D. "Miss Grayson looks like a kid herself. How does she rate a phone?"

"Get serious, Palmer," laughed Lisa. "Miss Grayson is a teacher. Of course she has a phone."

The girls plopped themselves down in their front sitting room. "You know what?" said Amy. "I'm starved. I didn't eat anything at the party. All those little sandwiches looked too boring."

"Let's order pizza!" Lisa exclaimed. "It's the night for the za-wagon."

"I'll call," Shanon volunteered. "There's a pay phone on this floor and I know the number by heart." The za-wagon was what the Alma girls called the Figaro's Pizza delivery truck. Since she was a local, Shanon had been ordering from them for years. "Let's get the Monstro. It has everything on it."

As soon as Shanon had collected money from each of the

4

girls and bolted out the door, Amy went into her bedroom to change. She unbuttoned her skirt with a sigh of relief. At least they could dress as they pleased in their own suite, she thought as she put on her black tights and black T-shirt.

"Maybe I'll go out for chorus," Amy said, wandering back into the sitting room and picking up her guitar. "If they don't have any rock groups here, I might as well try classical."

Palmer had stretched out lazily on the pink loveseat. "I hope you're not going to play that thing now," she said when Amy settled onto the floor with her guitar.

"I'll strum softly," Amy said.

Amy was still strumming and Palmer was practically asleep when Shanon hurried in with a large pizza twenty minutes later. "Get it while it's hot," Shanon called, putting the pizza down on a small desk in the corner of the room.

"How are we supposed to eat this?" asked Palmer, gingerly lifting back the lid of the box. "We don't have any plates or napkins."

"I guess you'll just have to rough it, Palmer," laughed Amy. She ducked into the bedroom and returned with four pieces of notebook paper. "This should do," she said, handing them each one piece.

"Yuck," groaned Palmer, wrinkling her nose as she pulled a cheesy slice of pizza from the pie and plopped it down on the paper.

"Now *this* is food," said Lisa, licking a glob of tomato sauce from her thumb. "One thing Alma lacks is good food. That cafeteria is the pits."

"I'll tell you another thing Alma lacks," griped Palmer as she picked the mushrooms off her slice.

5

"What?" said Amy, looking up from her "plate."

"B-O-Y-S!" Palmer spelled out.

"What about them?" mumbled Amy, her mouth full of pizza.

Palmer smiled smugly. She had their undivided attention. "The trouble with Alma," she declared, "is that there aren't any."

"Okay, so there aren't any boys," said Amy. "Does that mean the whole place is a downer?"

"Oh," said Palmer, "I suppose you aren't interested in them."

"But . . . I am," Amy admitted. "I just hadn't thought about it."

"Well, think about it," said Palmer. "We're going to be here until we're at least seventeen. How are we going to date? *Who* are we going to date?"

Lisa tossed her long dark hair. "There must be a way to meet some guys," she said. Lisa sounded pretty cool, Shanon thought, but there was a worried look in her brown eyes.

"It will be kind of strange," said Shanon. "My grammar school had both boys and girls."

"Mine, too," said Amy. "But my dad thought single-sex education would be good for me."

"What do you mean?" asked Lisa.

"You know. If you go to school with just girls, then you won't be distracted by boys," Amy explained. "And you won't be tempted to act dumb just to make some boy feel more secure about you—that whole thing."

"It does sort of make sense," said Shanon.

"It's *non*-sense, you mean," Palmer grumbled. "Alma's more like a prison than a school."

6

"Oh, it isn't that bad, Palmer," said Amy. "They sure don't eat like this in prison."

"They don't have such good company, either," Lisa said with a smile.

"Okay," Palmer admitted. "We may be having fun right now, even without any boys. But just wait until we've ordered the Monstro twenty-five times and spent a dozen Saturday nights sitting right here staring at each other. You'll be bored to tears then—wait and see."

"I'll never be bored with Figaro's pizza," Shanon said, swallowing. "My whole family loves it. My sister Doreen used to go there on all her dates."

"What's with you and your sister Doreen?" Palmer snapped. "You must have mentioned her ten times in the last two days."

Shanon shrugged. "So what? I only talk about her because she has an interesting life. She's pretty and popular and she's always doing different things. She even dated a boy from Ardsley Academy, and they hardly ever go out with local public-school girls."

"Ardsley," Palmer sighed, leaning back and thinking about the all-boys school just a few miles away. "A treasure trove of cute boys all in one place." Palmer smoothed her long blond hair away from her face. "If I were dating an Ardsley boy, I certainly wouldn't go to Figaro's with him!"

"Oh, excuse us," teased Lisa. "Where *would* you go?"

Amy didn't give Palmer time to answer. "I'd go to a rock concert. Or maybe ice-skating like I did with this adorable guy last winter."

Lisa choked. "You went on a date? A real date? You must have been only twelve then."

"I was. My family was vacationing in Switzerland. He was the son of a friend of my father's. When a bunch of us went skating, he paired off with me."

"Just a minute," Palmer said, taking another slice. "Do you mean you weren't by yourselves?"

Amy nodded. "It was a group date."

"Sorry," said Palmer. "That doesn't qualify. A date is when you go out alone with a boy, like I did."

"Wow!" said Shanon. "You went out on a real date—by yourself! When? Where?"

Palmer smiled. "I had just turned thirteen. We went to my mother's country club."

Amy stretched out on the floor and rested her hands on her stomach. "Boy, am I full! What did you eat there?"

"Lobster," Palmer announced proudly.

"How about dessert?" asked Lisa.

"Chocolate milkshakes," Palmer replied.

"Oh, gross me out!" cried Amy. "Lobster and milkshakes!"

Palmer lifted her chin haughtily. "My date and I happened to like milkshakes. And my mother said to order whatever we liked, no matter how much it cost."

"You mean your date didn't pay for you? Your mother did?" asked Lisa.

"It was no big deal," said Palmer. "All she had to do was sign for it."

"How could she sign for it if she wasn't there?" Shanon asked.

"She . . . she was," Palmer stammered. "She was at the next table, but—"

The other girls began to laugh. "No buts," Lisa informed her. "If your mother was with you, it doesn't qualify as a real date."

8

"No way. Doesn't rate at all," Amy agreed.

Palmer's face flushed. "Well, you can laugh all you like," she sulked. "How many dates have you been on, Lisa?"

"None of your business," said Lisa. "I wasn't the one who brought up the subject."

There was a hot moment of silence as the girls finished their pizza. "Don't worry," Shanon finally said. "We'll all have dates soon. There are lots of dances at Ardsley Academy. I heard about them from Doreen."

"I heard about them too," Lisa said, "from my brother Reggie, who goes there. But you have to be invited."

"What about the dances here at Alma?" Amy asked.

Lisa gave a thumbs-down sign. "Reggie told me about those, too. They're horrible. Everybody just stands around leaning against the wall. The boys from Ardsley come over on a bus, but the only girls they dance with are the ones they already know."

Palmer looked interested. "You mean some girls arrange dates with Ardsley boys?"

"I guess so," Lisa said with a shrug.

"I once had a boyfriend," Shanon said shyly.

Palmer sat up. "But that's impossible. You're so . . . so young."

"No, I'm not," said Shanon. "In a few months I'll be thirteen, just like you. People always say I look young for my age."

"Tell us about your boyfriend," said Amy, picking up her guitar and strumming lightly.

"Well," sighed Shanon, "it was this boy at my old school. His name was Arthur Stuart. We used to pass notes to each other. Once he drew a heart with our initials and passed it over to me. He even held my hand on the way home from school."

9

Lisa's brown eyes went wide. "Cool. I would give anything for something like that to happen."

"You can bet it won't happen here," Palmer said.

Lisa stuck her tongue out at Palmer. "You never know."

Amy put down her guitar and wandered into Lisa and Shanon's bedroom. "Mind if I put a CD on your player?" she called out to Lisa.

"Go ahead," Lisa answered. "How about some—" But her request was drowned out by the raucous music of Joan Jett blaring from the bedroom. "CD is incredible!" Amy shouted over the music as she returned to the sitting room. "This is much better than my Walkman."

At that moment there was a loud knock at the door. "What's all this noise?" asked Kate Majors, sticking her head in. Kate was a fifth-former in charge of the floor. She had long, straight mousy-colored hair and thick glasses, but she carried herself with an air of great self-importance.

Amy ran into Lisa and Shanon's room and turned the CD off. "That's better," Kate said primly. "Your lights should be out now too. It's past ten o'clock."

"But it's Saturday night," moaned Palmer.

"As dorm monitor I must warn you that breaking rules of any sort results in demerits," Kate said crossly. "And when you get demerits, you lose privileges."

"We're sorry, Kate," said Shanon. "We were getting ready for bed anyway."

"That's a good idea," said Kate, backing out the door without saying good night.

"What a stick-in-the-mud," huffed Palmer, flouncing toward her bedroom.

"Palmer," said Amy, "before you go to bed would you

10

do me a favor? Just say one positive thing about something or someone."

Palmer looked at Amy with a raised eyebrow. "Okay. Alma is great and I don't care if I never see a boy again for the next four years. Happy?"

"Come on, Palmer," said Lisa. "It's not all that bad. I'm sure we'll manage to meet some boys eventually."

"How?" Palmer asked. "By putting an ad in the paper?"

"Now *that* would be really wild," Amy said with a laugh.

"It would be really weird!" added Shanon.

"I'm beat," said Lisa, yawning. "I'm going to bed."

"Me, too," agreed Palmer, sailing out of the room. Amy trailed behind her.

Back in their own room, Lisa and Shanon changed into their nightshirts, switched off the light, and climbed into bed.

"You know what," Lisa spoke in the dark room. "I hate to admit it, but Palmer may be right about the boy problem. I've never had a date yet and it looks like I may not have one for a long, long time!"

"Well, at least you won't be the only one," said Shanon. "It looks like we're all going to be dateless for a while."

"There's got to be a way," Lisa muttered, "a way of beating the system."

Shanon snuggled down in her bed. "Why don't you sleep on it?"

"That's just what I'm going to do," said Lisa, pulling her quilt up to her chin. "I'm going to figure a way out of this."

CHAPTER TWO

"Why did nature invent prunes, anyway?" Palmer muttered as the girls stood in line for Monday-morning breakfast.

"They're only dried-up plums," said Amy, grabbing a fruit cup. Lisa and Shanon were just ahead of her, where the apple-cheeked English cook and dietician was dishing out the main courses from behind the counter. Mrs. Worth had been feeding the boarders at Alma Stephens for twenty-five years, and an earlier generation of Alma girls had given her the affectionate nickname "Mrs. Butter," after Mrs. Butterworth's pancake syrup.

"I'd like some pancakes and waffles, please," Lisa told Mrs. Butter.

"Have some oatmeal, too, love," Mrs. Butter urged, smiling. "It'll stick to your ribs more."

"I don't want anything sticking to my ribs," Palmer announced as she pushed past Lisa and the starches. "I'll have one soft-boiled egg if you don't mind."

Mrs. Butter lifted a critical eyebrow.

"Wait until you hear the incredible idea I have," Lisa said, whisking up her laden tray and turning back to her friends.

"What is it?" asked Shanon, grabbing a small box of dry cereal.

"I'll tell you all at the table," Lisa said mysteriously as the girls headed off to the bustling dining room. "Take the table by the window," Lisa instructed them. "It has only four chairs. That way we'll be alone."

"Why don't you want anyone to sit with us?" asked Amy.

Lisa grinned. "Because I have something confidential to tell you. It's about the boy problem." The girls set their trays down on the table. "What is it?" asked Palmer eagerly.

"Not so loud," cautioned Lisa, reaching into her burgundy book bag and pulling out a folded piece of paper. "The answer to our boy shortage is right here," she whispered, handing the paper to Shanon.

"I can't believe this," Shanon said, barely able to breathe. She passed the piece of paper on to Amy.

Amy took a quick look and chuckled. "This is unreal."

Palmer snatched it and began reading aloud. " 'Wanted: four boys for four girls at Alma seeking social life. Write to us and we'll write to you. Contact Lisa McGreevy, Palmer Durand, Amy Ho, and Shanon Davis in care of Fox Hall, Suite 3-D!' What is this? You've got to be kidding!"

Amy began laughing. "I think it's spectacular. I never would have thought of anything like this!"

"But to put our names on it . . ." said Shanon nervously.

"I'm not putting *my* name on it!" Palmer declared.

"Shhh!" said Lisa. "Do you want the whole world to hear?"

"Well, if you put up a sign like this, the whole world *will* hear about it!" Palmer insisted.

"Okay," said Lisa, "maybe we shouldn't use our real names."

"Where were you going to hang the notice?" asked Shanon.

Lisa laughed. "I wasn't going to hang a notice. I was going to put an ad in the Ardsley Academy newspaper for the boys to write to us."

"Oh," said Amy. "I get it. Like dates—only on paper?"

"Sort of," said Lisa, "but more like pen pals. Don't you see? It's a great way to meet boys! I actually got the idea from you and Shanon."

"From us?" Amy said, confused.

"Sure. You told me you still write to your old friends in England and Australia," Lisa explained. "And Shanon used to write notes to that boy in her old school. So, when Palmer made that crack about putting an ad in the newspaper. . . ."

"This is too much!" Palmer exclaimed. "It's ridiculous! I don't want any part in it!"

"Well, well, well—if it isn't the noisy bunch," a voice sang out. Kate Majors stood over them, carefully balancing a messy tray. She'd already finished her breakfast. As Kate put the tray down on their table, Palmer wrinkled her nose at the leftover oatmeal and discarded prune pits in her bowl.

"Hi, Kate," said Lisa, hastily putting the paper away. "Were we being too noisy?"

"I was referring to Saturday night," Kate said. "I also think I should remind you about the dress code here."

"We're wearing skirts," Amy grunted. "What more do they want?"

"It's not just wearing a skirt that matters," Kate informed them. "The faculty around here is very picky. And Miss Pryn is practically Victorian, though I for one think

14

she's a great headmistress. A lot of girls, especially third-formers, try to take advantage of the code, that's all. And I don't want any of the girls in my dorm to be among them."

"What's wrong with the way we're dressed?" asked Lisa.

"That skirt is rather short, don't you think?" said Kate, nodding toward Lisa's red jeans skirt.

Lisa smoothed down her skirt. "All my hems are this length," she told Kate.

"I suggest you let them down, then," said Kate stiffly.

"My skirt isn't short," protested Amy. "I can't see how I'm breaking the dress code."

Kate looked at her sourly. She studied Amy's long, baggy black sweatshirt dress, which was worn over black tights and black lace-up boots. "Technically you're not, but I don't think Miss Pryn would consider an all-black ensemble appropriate schoolwear."

Palmer looked down at her straight blue skirt and pale pink blouse. "I look okay, don't I?" she asked.

"Your clothes are fine, but there is a rule about makeup," Kate informed her.

"I'm not wearing any makeup!" Palmer lied.

Kate merely raised a skeptical eyebrow. "I don't mean to insult your natural beauty," she said sarcastically, "but it looks to me as if you're wearing mascara, blush, *and* eyeshadow."

Palmer colored with annoyance. "All right, I may have put a touch of makeup on," she admitted. "I didn't think anyone could tell."

"What about me?" asked Shanon timidly.

Kate smiled at her. Shanon was wearing a simple brown

15

skirt and a white button-down shirt. "You look fine," she said, picking up her tray and starting to leave. But then she suddenly turned back and added, "By the way, Shanon, Miss Grayson told me you were interested in working on the paper. I'm the assistant editor. I checked with the editor, Dolores, and she said it was fine if you wanted to be a gofer."

Shanon's face lit up. "I'd love to!" she said. "There's just one thing. What *is* a gofer?"

"It's someone who goes for anything we need. *Go-fer,* get it? It's not very glamorous work. In fact, it's the least exciting newspaper job there is," Kate explained.

"I don't care," Shanon said cheerfully. "I'd do anything to be part of *The Ledger* staff."

"Great," said Kate. "You'll be working with me most of the time. Come over to *The Ledger* office after classes today, why don't you?"

"Sure," said Shanon. "I'll be there."

Kate nodded. "And the rest of you read the dress code," she said before heading off to class.

"What a dweeb," Palmer seethed the minute Kate was out of earshot. "Kate Majors is just jealous!"

"I don't think so," said Shanon. "She just doesn't want us to get into trouble. Anyway, she can't be all bad. She's letting me be a gofer for *The Ledger*!"

"That's really incredible," said Amy.

"Yeah, congratulations," added Palmer. "It's great."

Shanon smiled at her suitemates and then looked at the clock on the cafeteria wall. "Wow! It's almost nine o'clock. We'd better get going or we'll be late for class."

The girls snatched up their books and hurried toward the door. As they entered the busy hallway, Shanon turned

16

to Lisa and said, "I'm so excited about working on the paper I don't know how I'm going to sit through my classes this morning."

"You'll manage," Lisa said flatly.

"Hey, what's the matter?" Shanon asked. "You look sort of bummed. Did Kate depress you?"

"No. I'm just disappointed that nobody liked my idea," Lisa said.

"Sorry. I guess we weren't very receptive," Shanon admitted. "It did sound sort of goofy, but, really, it might be fun."

Lisa flashed a smile. "Thanks. We'll talk later."

All four girls had biology together, and then Amy went off to advanced math while the other three went to Latin class. They met again for lunch in the cafeteria but had no chance to talk privately. There was assigned seating during lunch and they were placed at a table with Miss Grayson and a girl from their floor named Brenda.

"So, how are your classes?" Miss Grayson asked when they'd all been served.

"I'm concerned about the frog we're supposed to dissect in biology," said Palmer. "The day they cut him up I'm going to be absent."

"I know how you feel," Miss Grayson said with a laugh.

"I'm definitely trying out for chorus," Amy told them. "And I love my math class."

Miss Grayson smiled. "Terrific. How about you, Lisa?"

"I was wondering," Lisa ventured. "Is there ever any time when we have joint classes with the boys from Ardsley?"

Miss Grayson shook her head. "I'm afraid this is a young ladies' school all the way down the line."

"Look," said Brenda, her hands flying up to adjust the bow in her frizzy blond hair, "there's Mr. Griffith!"

Shanon took a deep breath and Lisa smothered a giggle, but Palmer kept her eyes on Miss Grayson. Two faint red spots appeared on the teacher's cheeks. "I'll see you later, girls," Miss Grayson said, breezing away. "Mr. Griffith and I have a conference."

"Did you see how she blushed?" Palmer whispered.

"I don't blame her," Amy sighed. "He's *so* cute!"

"I can't tell whether his eyes are brown or green," said Palmer. "They're really unusual, though!"

"They're definitely green," Amy pronounced.

"No, I think they're brown," said Palmer.

"You just said you couldn't tell what color they were," Amy pointed out.

"Maybe they're hazel," Shanon offered. "Anyway, whatever you call them, they're definitely gorgeous."

"Definitely," Lisa agreed. "At least Miss Grayson thinks so."

"The whole school knows they like each other," Brenda gossiped. "Wouldn't it be something if they got married!"

"Wow," said Lisa. "That would be so romantic."

"And here we are—not even able to get dates," huffed Palmer. "Fat chance *we'll* ever be married."

Amy laughed. "Maybe some of us don't want to get married. Of course, those of us who do could always use Lisa's idea, but advertise for husbands instead—"

Lisa kicked Amy beneath the table.

"What are you talking about?" asked Brenda.

"Nothing," Amy replied, trying to keep a straight face.

"If you think the boy problem is heavy now," Brenda snorted, "wait until you're fourteen like I am."

"I hear the dances here are really awful," Palmer drawled.

"I'll enjoy them this year," Brenda said, getting up from the table with a smile. "Because this year I've got a boyfriend who goes to Ardsley."

Palmer looked after Brenda jealously as she walked away. "Did you hear that? She's got a real boyfriend. I wonder how she met him."

"Maybe she put an ad in the paper," Shanon quipped.

"You can laugh now," said Lisa, "but someday you'll wish *we'd* done that."

"I actually do think it's worth considering," said Amy. "It might be fun."

"Not me," said Palmer stubbornly.

After lunch, Shanon went to meet Kate in the *Ledger* office while Lisa went to check out the art studio. Amy headed for the language lab—she had elected to take Spanish instead of French—and Palmer returned to the suite to take a nap before French class.

Shanon arrived at the newspaper office just as Kate was on her way out. "I thought you were coming later on," Kate said briskly. "I'm off to calculus now."

"Calculus?" gasped Shanon. "You must be a brain."

"No, I'm not," said Kate. "I'm just a hard worker. You're the one who's really brainy."

"Me?"

"You're here on full scholarship, aren't you? And you're only twelve!"

"I'm good at some things," Shanon said with a shrug. She hesitated in the doorway, peering wistfully through the glass.

Kate looked at her watch. "I guess I've got five minutes

to show you around. Come on in. The door's always unlocked."

"Thanks," said Shanon, stepping inside.

"How are you at computers?" Kate asked, walking over to a shiny PC in the corner.

"Okay, I guess," Shanon said uncertainly. "But I've never used this kind before."

"I'll show you how to operate it," Kate offered.

Shanon eyed the fancy electric typewriter on the other side of the room. It looked as new as the computer. But she was relieved to see that the rest of the office was comfortably old-fashioned. The walls were covered with framed editions of old *Ledgers,* some dating way back to the 1920s. And the two long wooden tables and desks looked almost as old. One table was strewn with photographs and preliminary layouts. Another had a series of baskets containing typed manuscripts. An old file cabinet painted green stood by the window, and some shelves near the ceiling were crowded with cameras, lenses, and film cans.

"We don't have very much space, as you can see," Kate said.

"I think it's wonderful," breathed Shanon.

Kate perched on the edge of a desk. "A lot of the class reporters work from their rooms, and then Dolores and I go over their stuff. I like working here, myself."

Shanon sighed. "I don't blame you. How do you get to be a class reporter?" she asked.

"I'm afraid Dolores doesn't believe in admitting new girls to the writing staff," Kate told her. "Sorry. There have been third-form writers in the past, but since Dolores is the editor, she sets the policy this year."

Shanon's eyes drifted along one of the tables to the copy in the baskets. "Just exactly what does a gofer do?"

"Take stuff to the printer, pick up copy, type—that kind of thing. And you might have to do some mailings to the locals. We try to hit them for advertising."

"I know a lot of the people who run the stores around here," Shanon said eagerly. "My father owns a garage not far away."

"Great," said Kate. "Maybe he can put an ad in *The Ledger*. Oh, yes, another thing—you'll have to sort the mail. Dolores doesn't like doing it herself."

"Sure, I can handle that," said Shanon. "You want me to do it in the morning?"

"Good idea," said Kate. "The postmistress, Ginger, drops it off at around seven-thirty. Dolores and I don't usually get to the office until ten. We've both got an early Greek class."

"Okay," said Shanon. "Anything else?"

"The floor could use a sweep in the morning. It could use one right now, come to think of it."

"Okay," Shanon said. "Where's the broom?"

"Next to the file cabinet," Kate said, glancing down at her watch again. "I have to run now. See you later," she called, shutting the door behind her.

Shanon picked up the broom and looked around the messy little office. *Oh, well,* she thought cheerfully, *I've got to start somewhere. . . .*

"This has been the longest, most boring day of my life! First those disgusting frogs and—"

Amy rolled her eyes at Palmer. "Will you shut up a minute."

21

"Will you stop telling me what to do!" Palmer snapped.

"I'm trying to tune my guitar," Amy insisted. "I have to learn this music for quartet trials."

"Quartet trials," Palmer laughed scornfully. "What are you singing?"

Amy groaned. "Some kind of Bach."

"Bach?" squealed Palmer.

Amy frowned. "Don't laugh. It's the chorus or nothing. That's the only place a person can do any singing around here."

"But you don't have the voice for that kind of stuff," insisted Palmer. "I've heard you in the shower."

"Just leave me alone." Amy began humming loudly.

"Listen to this!" Lisa said eagerly, running into the sitting room. "I've thought of a way to put in the ad. We'll use code names!"

"Don't tell me you're still on that topic," laughed Palmer just as Shanon came bursting into the room.

"Sorry I'm late," she said, kicking off her shoes. "I went to the bookstore." Leaving Palmer and Lisa sitting on the loveseat and Amy sprawled on the floor, she went straight into the bedroom and examined her apricot blouse and green skirt in the mirror.

"Can I borrow some of your clothes?" Shanon called out to Lisa. "Now that we're out of class, I'd like to forget the dress code. But all my clothes are so normal. . . ."

"Take anything you like!" yelled Lisa. "Just get back out here! I've thought of another way to get pen pals!"

Shanon laughed. "Don't you ever give up?!" Rummaging through Lisa's drawer, she pulled out a pair of red harem pants and put them on with her own blouse. "These are really strange," she giggled, coming out of the room. "Where did you get them?"

"My mom let me buy them in New York," Lisa told her. "These, too," she added, pointing to the blue velvet knickers and cropped shirt she was wearing.

"What about the ad?" asked Amy, changing the subject.

Lisa smiled. "At last I've got *somebody* interested."

"Of course we're interested," said Palmer cautiously. "But that doesn't mean we're going to do it."

"Well, let's say that we did put an ad in the Ardsley paper," Lisa began again. "If we used a code name, nobody would have to know it was us."

Amy nodded. "A code name, huh? I like that."

"There are a couple of choices," Lisa said, scribbling in her notebook. "What do you think of Amli Palsha or Shamy Lipa."

Amy's mouth dropped open. "Amli Palsha?"

"Shamy Lipa?" gasped Palmer.

"They're combinations of all our names." Lisa shrugged. "Just a try."

"I know what," Amy said. "Let's make up an underground-sounding code name—like Lipstick or The Terrors."

Palmer rolled her eyes. "The Terrors? I'm not going to call myself that."

"Well, what *would* you call yourself?" Lisa prodded. "If you were going to do it, that is."

Palmer thought for a moment. "How about Pandora?" she suggested. "Like in Pandora's box?"

"No, that sounds too frightening," said Amy. "What we need is something that makes us sound cool."

"Excuse *me*," muttered Palmer.

"How about the Foxes?" Shanon said suddenly. "I mean . . . we do live in Fox Hall!"

Palmer's eyes lit up. "The Foxes—I think that fits us perfectly."

"It's great," Lisa said, "but I don't think it's enough. We need something more—something mysterious."

"I know," cried Amy. "Foxes of the Third Dimension!"

"That's great!" said Shanon. "Where'd you get the third dimension part? It sounds really intelligent."

"From our suite number!" Amy told her. "3-D!"

"Wow!" said Palmer. "That's heavy!"

Amy chuckled. "Wrong! It's not heavy—it's deep!"

"The third dimension is depth!" cried Lisa. "You're right! Incredible! What a super code name. It's us!"

"I agree," said Palmer. "It makes us sound pretty, intelligent, witty, charming, mysterious—all the things we are."

"Maybe we should write that down in the ad," giggled Lisa.

Shanon shook her head. "No, I don't think so. We don't want to sound conceited."

"And," Palmer added, "we don't want to attract the wrong kind of boys. I wonder if anyone will really answer us."

Lisa looked at her mischievously. "So, you actually want to do it?"

"I didn't say that," Palmer replied.

"How come?" challenged Lisa. "You're the one who's always talking about how awful it is without any boys at Alma."

"That's right," said Amy. "And now you don't want to go along with Lisa's idea."

"Maybe it's because you didn't think of it yourself," said Lisa.

Palmer's face reddened. "That's not it!"

"Well, then," said Amy impishly, "maybe you're just scared."

"I am not scared!" declared Palmer. "I could handle any boy any day. I have more experience than all of you put together."

"Then what's the problem? Why won't you go along with us?" asked Lisa.

Palmer hesitated a moment. "All right," she finally said. "Count me in. If somebody really does answer the ad, it might be a lot of fun. As long as it's a boy who's cute, smart, rich—"

"And tall," added Lisa, stretching out her long legs.

Amy giggled. "And he should definitely know karate and play in a rock band!"

"I can't believe we're actually doing this," said Shanon.

"We haven't done anything yet," said Palmer. "What are we waiting for? Let's write up the ad and mail it to the *Ardsley Lion* newspaper. Is that all there is to it?"

"That's the plan," said Lisa. "How about this? . . . 'Wanted: boys who can write four lonely hearts at Alma.' "

"Who wants boys?" laughed Palmer. "Let's say, 'Wanted: real men.' "

Shanon covered her face. "Oh, we couldn't!"

Amy strummed her guitar and howled like a coyote. "Oh, we are just lonely cowgirls, lookin' for some hunky cowhands," she sang with a country-western twang.

"No way, no cowboys," said Palmer, wrinkling her nose. "Someone much more charming, please."

"I know, you'd like somebody who showed up in a

tuxedo," Lisa teased. "And a top hat, white gloves, and a cane."

"That would be okay," agreed Palmer.

Amy stood up ramrod straight and held a folded piece of paper to her neck as if it were a bow tie. "Good evening," she said in a mincing voice, pretending to be Palmer's dream date. "I am Richard Rich-boy, here to collect Princess Palmer Durand. The Rolls Royce is outside."

Lisa and Shanon screamed with laughter. Palmer jumped up and grabbed Amy's guitar. "I'm Ricky the Rocker—ya date fer tunite," she growled, scratching her belly. "That's the kind of guy you'd like, Amy."

Shanon and Lisa were helpless with laughter. "We'd better calm down," said Lisa, holding her side. "Otherwise Kate's going to come knocking on the door."

"Maybe we should let Kate in on it," Palmer giggled. " 'Wanted: one sourpuss boy who will find perfect match at Alma.' "

"Get serious a minute," said Shanon, who had taken a piece of paper from her notebook. "How about this? 'Wanted: boys who can write. Alma girls against single-sex education seek boy pen pals from Ardsley Academy. Send letters to Foxes of the Third Dimension, Alma Stephens School for Girls.' "

"Hey," said Lisa, "that sounds almost real."

"It *is* real," said Shanon. "I thought you were serious about wanting to try this."

"We are," said Lisa. "After all, it's just a goof, like Amy said. And if it works . . ."

"If it works," exclaimed Palmer, "we'll all have boys to invite to the dances!"

"Yeah," said Amy. "We'll have dates."

Lisa smiled. "Incredible. And at the very least, we might meet some interesting people. Boys can be good company when they want to be."

"If they're not drips," Palmer warned. "How are we going to avoid that part?"

Lisa shrugged. "We're the ones putting in the ad. It's up to us to read their letters and decide whether they're drips or not."

"Uh-oh," said Amy. "I just thought of something. If we don't give the boys our real names, how will they know where to send their letters?"

"That's right," said Palmer. "It can't be here. If they address everything to Suite 3-D, everyone will know we're the Foxes."

"Unless . . ." Shanon said softly. "One of my jobs at *The Ledger* is to sort through the mail in the morning. The postmistress leaves it in the office first thing. And Kate and Dolores are never there that early."

Lisa's eyes opened wider. "Perfect!"

After adding one more line to the ad, Shanon re-read it:

WANTED: BOYS WHO CAN WRITE
ALMA GIRLS AGAINST SINGLE-SEX EDUCATION SEEK BOY PEN PALS FROM ARDSLEY ACADEMY. SEND LETTERS TO FOXES OF THE THIRD DIMENSION IN CARE OF ALMA STEPHENS LEDGER, ALMA STEPHENS SCHOOL FOR GIRLS.

Everyone roared. "Yaay Foxes!" cried Lisa.

A thump was heard on the ceiling. "Lights out!" a voice commanded through the walls. The four Foxes smiled at one another, and for a moment they were quiet.

27

CHAPTER THREE

"Hey, everybody," Amy called, bounding into the sitting room. "I made the chorus!"

Lisa unwrapped the towel from her freshly washed hair. "That's fantastic!"

"It's unbelievable, you mean," added Palmer, looking up from her toenails, which she was busy painting a pale, pearly pink.

Amy shrugged modestly. "I didn't get all the notes right in the quartet trials, but the director said he liked my enthusiasm. I also think they needed tenors."

"No doubt," Palmer said. "Not many girls have such deep voices."

Amy disappeared into her bedroom for a minute and came out with her math book.

"Don't tell me you're going to try to study out here," Palmer complained. "It's bad enough we have to talk softly because Shanon is reading in the corner. This is supposed to be a sitting room, not a library."

"I'm done," Shanon piped up, leaving the desk. Amy took her place and plopped down her books.

"Come on, Amy, study in the bedroom," Palmer grumbled.

"How can I?" Amy replied. "The desk in our room is totally covered with your stuff."

At that moment there was a knock on the door. "Is Shanon here?" trilled a tall, slim girl with large brown eyes and cascades of wavy auburn hair.

"Hi, Shanon," said Dolores Countee, smiling radiantly as she stepped inside. "I just wanted to tell you what a great job you're doing as a gofer. Sorry I'm hardly ever there. But Kate says she's pleased."

"Thanks," Shanon said, blushing.

"How are things working out with you and Kate?" Dolores asked, tossing a lock of hair back from her face.

"Okay," Shanon answered.

"Glad to hear it. Kate can be a grump, but she's okay underneath. And of course she's been even worse this year. I think the thing with that boy from Ardsley last spring really soured her. He was such a—" Dolores stopped herself in mid-sentence, blushing prettily. "Oh, well, I shouldn't gossip. Got to run."

"Bye," said Shanon. "Thanks again for stopping by."

"Well, well," said Palmer as soon as the door was closed again. "The great Dolores Countee came by just to see you. What an honor!"

"I think it was nice of her," Shanon protested.

"It's also about the most exciting thing that's happened around here in the last two weeks," Amy added.

"I know," said Palmer. "So much for the Foxes of the Third Dimension. It's been two weeks, and not a single boy has sent us a letter."

"It must have been that ad, Shanon," Palmer.

"What was wrong with it?" Lisa demanded.

"It made us sound too smart," Palmer said. "All that stuff about single-sex education made us sound like bookworms. Boys don't like that."

29

Shanon looked hurt. "How do you know?"

"Because Palmer knows everything," Amy muttered sarcastically.

There was another knock at the door. Lisa went to open it, and Maggie Grayson came in. She was wearing a lavender dress and carrying a newspaper under her arm.

"Sorry to disturb you, girls," Miss Grayson said. "But I've been asked by Miss Pryn to canvass the dorm. Something has come to our attention. . . ." And she held up the newspaper. It was the *Ardsley Lion*.

"It seems that a group of girls has placed a rather unusual ad in the Ardsley paper," Miss Grayson continued.

Shanon threw timid glances at Lisa and Amy, whose faces were expressionless. Palmer had ducked her head and was busy putting her boots on.

"Miss Pryn wants to get to the bottom of the mystery," said Miss Grayson. "Would you happen to know who the Foxes of the Third Dimension are?"

Shanon started to shake inside.

"Why?" Lisa blurted out. "Are they in trouble?"

"Heavens, I hope not," Miss Grayson said. "But Miss Pryn is rather touchy about the school's reputation, and the ad has created quite a stir over at Ardsley. It's gotten back to us through some of the teachers there. Several of the boys are writing to these girls. In any case, the impression it's giving—"

"You mean they're writing letters?" Amy exclaimed.

Palmer gave Amy a warning look. "I've never heard anything about any Foxes of the Third Dimension," she said. "If you ask me, it's the stupidest thing I've ever heard of."

"I wouldn't go that far," said Miss Grayson. "But it is something the headmistress would like to check out."

"Well, if we hear anything, we'll let you know," Palmer volunteered. Lisa, Shanon, and Amy stared open-mouthed at her.

"Thanks," said Miss Grayson as she went out the door. "I'm sure it's just a tempest in a teapot."

"I hope so," squeaked Shanon.

Lisa got up and shut the door again. This time she looked petrified. "What have we done?" she exclaimed. "We're going to get into a lot of trouble."

"I don't see how," said Amy.

"Right," said Palmer. "No one knows it was us."

"And that's another thing," Lisa fumed. "Who told you to lie for all of us, Palmer Durand?"

"I'm not having a run-in with Miss Pryn," Palmer shot back. "Not over some stupid pen pal ad, anyway. My mother will cancel my charge accounts."

"Your charge accounts?" breathed Shanon. "What about my scholarship?"

"Let's not get carried away," said Amy. "Nobody actually said we broke a rule. And if we did, what could it be?"

"Nothing," Lisa said thoughtfully. "There couldn't be a rule against writing letters. Miss Pryn's probably just touchy about the 'single-sex' business."

Shanon hung her head. "That was my idea. Sorry. Well, anyway it *is* a tempest in a teapot, just like Miss Grayson said. We put the ad in but we didn't get a single letter."

"Wait a minute," said Amy. "Miss Grayson said that the ad created a stir at Ardsley."

"And that boys were writing," added Palmer.

Lisa turned to Shanon. "Have you been checking the mail at *The Ledger* every morning?"

"Every morning," she answered. "I'm always the first one there, except for Ginger. She leaves the mail on Dolores's desk and then I sort it."

"That's it!" said Palmer. "It's the postmistress! Ginger must be stealing our mail."

Lisa laughed. "That's crazy. Ginger is married and has two children. Why would she want a pen pal from Ardsley?"

"Can we talk about this later?" said Amy. "I've got to knock out these trig problems now. I have a chorus rehearsal tonight."

"Sure," said Lisa. "Your first rehearsal—good luck."

"Thanks. I'll need it. I'm having trouble reading the music. I've always played by ear with the guitar."

"Excuse me," said Shanon. "I'm going in to our room. I want to start my English paper on *Great Expectations*."

"Already?" griped Palmer. "It isn't due for weeks. You're just going to make the rest of us look bad."

"Sorry," Shanon said meekly. "The book just got me excited."

"Don't mind Palmer," Lisa said, trailing behind her. "I'll go in with you. Those Latin vocabulary words have me stymied. I'd like it more if I could speak it."

Shanon laughed. "You probably would." She glanced at Lisa. Her roommate looked thoughtful. "Don't worry. You'll get the hang of it."

Lisa smiled. "I wasn't thinking about Latin. I was thinking about our pen pal ad. I wonder if some guys really did send letters. And if they did, where are they?"

The next morning Shanon went to the newspaper office earlier than usual. She could hardly wait to check the mail. But she was so early that Ginger hadn't delivered it yet. There was no stack of envelopes on Dolores's big, cluttered desk. Wandering over to the wooden drafting table, Shanon checked the layout for the next issue. The front-page story was about the Alma soccer team. Then she snooped around on Kate's desk to see what copy she had collected from the class reporters. On top of the pile was a story about the new chem lab; then there was an article on Miss Pryn's Opening Day speech. Shanon tried to remember it—something about ethics. There was even a little blurb about the third-form get-acquainted party. There was nothing, Shanon noticed, about the world outside Alma; nothing about the politics of the school. For the first time she realized that *The Ledger* was rather dull reading. But that didn't matter. Working on any kind of newspaper was exciting enough.

"Hi, Shanon."

Shanon turned quickly as Kate entered the office. In her hand was a big stack of envelopes.

"Hi," Shanon replied. "Is that the mail?"

Kate nodded and leafed through the stack.

"I thought you had Greek class," Shanon said, flustered.

Kate peered at her. "I do. Ginger's out sick with the flu, so I've been stopping at Booth Hall to pick up our mail."

"Oh," Shanon said. "I could have done that."

"I know," said Kate. "But I think Dolores and I have you running around enough. The newspaper office is on my way to Greek, so I decided to—" Kate's voice broke off suddenly as she lifted two letters out of the stack and stalked to her desk. "Ah-ha!" she exclaimed. "Two more!"

"Wh-what is it?" Shanon stuttered, peering over Kate's shoulder.

"Never mind," said Kate. "I don't think I should talk about it. Not until I speak with Miss Pryn, anyway."

"Miss Pryn?" Shanon gulped as she caught sight of the letter on top. It was addressed to Foxes of the Third Dimension in care of the Alma *Ledger*.

"Foxes of the Third Dimension," Shanon said softly. "I think I. . . ."

"You what?" Kate demanded, turning around. "If you find out who they are, you'd better stay away from them. They're going to be in big trouble."

"They are?" squeaked Shanon. "Why?"

Kate opened the bottom drawer of her desk and pulled out a thick manila folder that was stuffed with mail. "It's too complicated to explain," she told Shanon, sticking the two letters into the folder. "I'd better not leave these here," she muttered. "We'll need them for evidence."

"Evidence?" Shanon said, panic tightening her throat. "Evidence about what?"

"Just count your lucky stars you don't know," Kate said grimly.

"It's probably just some sort of prank, don't you think?" said Shanon.

"Some prank!" Kate snorted. Stuffing the folder into her satchel, she gave Shanon a distracted wave and walked out the door.

Shanon sank into a chair, her stomach churning. What in the world had she gotten herself into?

"She said it's some kind of evidence!" Shanon wailed. Lisa, Amy, and Palmer were looking at Shanon with

34

puzzled expressions. All four girls were back in the suite getting ready for lunch.

"I never heard anything so silly in my whole life!" said Palmer. She tossed her head haughtily, but her blue eyes looked worried.

"We can't be in trouble," said Lisa, trying to convince herself.

"I'm not so sure," said Amy. "In any case, I suggest we get those letters."

"But we can't," Shanon faltered. "Kate has them."

"But she has no right to them," fumed Lisa. "They're ours."

"That's right," Palmer chimed in. "I know just what she's up to. She's trying to steal our pen pals, because she's too homely to get one herself."

"You really think she's trying to cash in on our idea?" Lisa said doubtfully.

Palmer gulped. "Well, what else could it be?"

"I'm not sure," Shanon sighed, "but it has something to do with Miss Pryn."

Lisa took a deep breath. "Then there's only one thing we can do. We've got to get those letters away from Kate—and if need be, destroy them."

"Maybe we should just confess," said Shanon. "Admit that we're the Foxes."

"And get in trouble?" said Palmer. "Not me!"

"Kate's going downstairs now," said Amy, peeking out the doorway. "She's wearing her jacket."

"Good. She must be going out," said Palmer. "This is our chance."

Shanon turned pale. "What are we going to do?"

"What do you think?" Lisa said, sounding determined. "Those letters are ours. Let's go get them!"

35

With Palmer as the lookout, they sneaked down to Kate's room. They were in luck—the door had been left open.

Shanon hung back from the others. "Maybe we shouldn't."

"Yeah, maybe we shouldn't," Amy agreed. "It's Kate's room."

"But it's our mail," Palmer insisted.

The four girls hesitated in the hallway. There was no one else in sight. Palmer nudged Lisa. "Go on in!"

With her dark eyes wide as saucers, Lisa slipped into the room. Palmer and Amy followed quickly; then came Shanon.

"Look!" Shanon gasped, pointing to the top of Kate's dresser. "They're here!" The other three girls gathered around her and stared at the big folder Shanon recognized from the newspaper office.

"Look how many letters there are," Palmer said, gaping.

"I think we'd better get out of here," Amy said, looking around. "If we get caught. . . ."

Lisa grabbed the folder and they all ran quickly down the hall to their suite.

"Whew!" breathed Lisa, shutting the door. "We made it!"

"And look at the loot," Palmer said, eyeing the letters. "Let's open them."

"Wait," Shanon gasped. "I . . . I think I left my pencil in Kate's room."

"So what?" said Amy.

"It was in my hair and then I was holding it. . . ."

"What's the big deal?" said Palmer.

Shanon trembled. "I left it . . . in Kate's room."

"Who cares?" said Lisa. "It's only a pencil."

"It's *not* just a pencil," moaned Shanon. "It's got the name of my father's garage on it."

"Oh, no," Lisa cried, "You'd better go get it."

"We'll tell you what's in the letters," Palmer added.

"We'll do no such thing," Lisa said, putting her foot down. "We'll wait until we're all here."

"That's right," said Amy. "Hurry, Shanon."

With her heart thumping, Shanon ran back to Kate's room—and bumped into Kate right outside the door.

"It's getting very chilly outside," Kate said, eyeing Shanon curiously. "I came back for my scarf. What are you doing here?"

Shanon stood dumbfounded in the doorway.

"What is it?" Kate asked, pushing past Shanon and into the room.

"I wanted to ask you . . . I wanted to write something for *The Ledger*," Shanon stammered, following Kate inside.

"Dolores is against third-form writers, I already told you," Kate said as she headed straight for the dresser. "Davis's Garage?" she mumbled, picking up Shanon's pencil. "Whose is this?"

"It's mine," Shanon confessed. "I was in here . . . waiting for you. I wanted to ask you . . ." She fished wildly for something to say that would explain the pencil—or at least distract Kate.

Suddenly Shanon's eye fell on a framed snapshot of a boy on the dresser. His face looked very familiar. "Who's that?" she asked. "I think I know him."

"Never mind," Kate said, her face turning red. "His name is Bob. He . . . he used to be a friend . . . kind of."

37

She pulled open the drawer and took out a scarf. Then she glanced down at the spot where the folder had been.

Just then, Shanon heard the voices of her suitemates coming down the hall. "Haven't you gotten your pencil yet?" Lisa blurted, walking right into Kate's room. "Come on, Shanon!"

"Otherwise, we're going to open them up without you," Palmer drawled, still out of sight.

Shanon winced and Kate's face got stony. Lisa just stood there with her mouth open—and the "evidence" in her hand.

"You!?" Kate sputtered, sizing things up as Palmer and Amy came into view. "I can't believe it!" She turned on Shanon. "I warned you." And snatching the folder from Lisa, she said, "I'll take those."

"But they're not addressed to you," Lisa argued.

"I'm the monitor in Fox Hall," Kate said coldly. "Until we get to the bottom of this, those letters belong to Miss Pryn."

"To the bottom of what?" asked Amy, beginning to look scared.

Kate stuck the folder under her arm and stalked by them. "I have to go. And so do you. I want you all out of my room right now, if you don't mind."

"No, we don't mind," Shanon faltered.

Kate gave her a parting glare and stormed out. Everyone followed sheepishly. "I never thought *you'd* get mixed up in something like this, Shanon," Kate called over her shoulder. She shook her head at the others. "The four Foxes, huh!"

CHAPTER FOUR

Everybody was nervous the morning the Foxes were called in to see Miss Pryn.

"What do you think she'll do to us?" Shanon asked in a worried voice. "If I get kicked out, my mom and dad will be so disappointed."

"We're not going to get kicked out," Lisa whispered, trying to sound confident.

"You can come in now, young ladies." Miss Pryn's secretary showed them in from the outer office. Palmer, Amy, Shanon, and Lisa stood in a line in front of the headmistress's big Victorian desk. Except for the get-acquainted party, this was as close as the girls had ever been to her. The tall, broad-shouldered woman with iron-gray hair had a reputation for being a strict disciplinarian.

Miss Pryn waved at the chairs along the wall. "Pull up some seats, young ladies," she said without a smile.

The girls dragged the cane chairs along the green carpet.

"Now. . . ." Miss Pryn paused and looked at each girl in turn. Her bright blue eyes seemed to bore right through them. "About these letters. . . ." She waved the folder full of envelopes in front of their faces.

"We have a tradition of openness here at Alma," Miss Pryn went on. "That's why we discourage this kind of activity."

39

Lisa, Shanon, Palmer, and Amy exchanged worried glances. Things were worse than they'd thought.

"What activity?" Lisa ventured.

"You know very well," said Miss Pryn crossly. "It seems that every year we have to stop girls from doing this."

"You do?" asked Lisa, shocked. "You mean girls do this all the time?"

"Of course they do," Miss Pryn answered. "They think it gives them prestige."

"We didn't think that, honest," Amy spoke up. "We just thought we'd get to meet some new people."

"And you'd exclude others," said Miss Pryn.

"We'd have to, don't you think?" said Palmer cautiously. "I mean, we couldn't write to everyone."

"That's just the point," Miss Pryn snapped. "You can't invite everyone, and so feelings are hurt."

The girls looked at one another. They weren't quite sure they were following Miss Pryn. "Invite everyone where?" asked Shanon timidly.

"Don't be coy with me, young lady," the headmistress scolded. "Invite them into your sorority, of course!"

"Sorority?" Lisa said.

"What sorority?" asked Palmer.

"I thought sororities were against the rules," added Amy.

Miss Pryn studied the girls skeptically. "Do you mean to tell me this isn't some sorority prank?"

"It's only the four of us," Lisa explained. "We just wanted to get some pen pals who are boys. We didn't mean to upset anybody or break any rules."

Miss Pryn let out a sigh. "Well, I never . . . What a

40

misunderstanding," she said. And then with a quiet chuckle, she added, "What an idea!"

"You mean it's okay?" Shanon asked, brightening.

"There's no law against putting an ad in the paper—or writing letters, for that matter," Miss Pryn said.

"Then it won't affect my scholarship?" Shanon added.

Miss Pryn's face softened. "Of course not." She paused for a moment. "Whether you realize it or not, we recognize the need for a coed social life here. That's why we give dances. In fact, there's one coming up in October."

"Maybe the dances aren't enough," Lisa ventured.

"Yes, maybe if we had an exchange program with the Ardsley boys . . ." Amy suggested.

"Or some kind of joint field trips," said Shanon.

"Or some phones in our rooms," Palmer piped up.

Miss Pryn put up a hand. "I get the idea," she said with a smile. "I'll keep your suggestions in mind."

"We didn't mean any harm," Lisa apologized.

"I can see that now," said Miss Pryn. "Actually, the idea is rather bold." Her eyes twinkled. "I think it's about time someone brought back the fine art of letter-writing."

Shanon, Palmer, Amy, and Lisa grinned at one another, then at Miss Pryn as she stood up at her desk and handed over the letters.

Bouncing onto Lisa's bed, the girls tossed the letters up into the air.

"Look at all these!" cried Lisa. "It's incredible."

"What are we waiting for?" exclaimed Palmer. "Let's open them up!" Everybody began grabbing wildly.

"Hold on!" said Lisa. "Let's open these one at a time and read them together. It'll be more fun."

41

"Okay," said Palmer, ripping the first one open. "Look at this!"

Dear Foxes,

I like your name. Does this mean you are foxy? I hope so. Write to me about your dreams.

Sigmund Freud

Lisa grabbed an envelope. "Let's open another one!"

Dear Foxes,

I am definitely an earth man and would like to correspond with you.

Moose Hansen

"I'm not going to write to anyone named Moose," said Amy. "He might have antlers. Better open another."

Dear Foxes,

The last thing we want to do is to write to a bunch of girls. That's why we go to Ardsley.

Ardsley Chapter of the W.H.C.

"What's that stand for?" Shanon asked.

"Woman Haters Club," explained Lisa. "I heard about it from Reggie."

"Ugh," said Palmer.

Amy picked up another letter. "Let's see what's next."

The girls continued to open the letters one at a time. Some were humorous:

Dear Foxie sisters,
  Your ad races my motor. If I had an airplane, I'd parachute over!

                                        Yours,
                                        Toadie

Others were serious:

My dear Foxes,
  It would be a great honor to correspond with you.

                                        Very truly yours,
                                        Bill Cody

But most of them were just boring! In fact, the most fascinating thing about them was the names of the letter-writers. Jaimie Wadsworth Longfellow IV, Bob Anklefoot, Joe Short, Compton Hughes III, Joe Sweetwater, Oliver Baron Jr., Lucas Fox, and Ahmad Dinnerstein.

"How are we ever going to decide between these?" moaned Palmer. "Nobody says anything personal. To think we almost got kicked out of school over these!"

"We should have asked the boys to say something about themselves in the letter," Shanon said softly.

Lisa groaned and stretched out on the bed. Letters were all around them. "There's one left," she said, handing the last envelope to Shanon. "You read it."

Shanon ripped open the envelope. The paper was dark red and the letter was written in calligraphy. "Hey, look at this handwriting! It's almost as good as Amy's!"

"Who cares about handwriting?" yawned Palmer. "What does it say?"

Dear Foxes of the Third Dimension,

Your idea is deep. We're suffocating at Ardsley also. In fact, we're dying. Revive us with your letters.

The Unknown
(four guys from Ardsley)

Lisa sat up. "Let me see that! Incredible—there are four of them, just like us!"

"You think it's for real?" asked Palmer.

"Of course it's for real!" Amy chirped. "They're just being mysterious like we were."

Lisa grinned. "I can't believe that 'revive us' part!"

"I don't know," said Palmer. "They didn't even give us their names. Where are we supposed to write to them?"

Lisa looked at the bottom of the letter. "It says here to send the answers to The Unknown in care of Kirby. That's the third-form dorm at Ardsley."

"That means they're the same age we are. Probably really goofy," said Palmer, disappointed.

"They don't sound goofy to me," said Amy.

"Me, either," said Lisa. "They're only using a code name like we did. And there are four of them! It's perfect!" She turned to Shanon. "What do you think?"

Shanon's face reddened up to the roots of her hair. "I think we should write them back," she said. "But we should ask them for their real names."

"We certainly should," said Palmer. "If they're going to be our pen pals, we need to know something about them. I don't want to get stuck writing to some creep. And how will we know what they look like?"

"Brother, you're all so picky!" Lisa complained. "This is the best letter we've gotten, and I agree with Shanon that we answer it. Unless you're scared to?" This last comment was directed at Palmer.

Palmer's face turned pink with annoyance—or embarrassment. "Me scared? How dare you!"

"Okay, then!" said Amy. She marched over to the desk and picked up Shanon's French notebook. "Mind if I tear out a piece of paper?"

"Wait!" said Palmer. She ran to her room and came back with some pink stationery. "I think this looks better. We can soak it in perfume."

"Gross," said Amy. "Why stink up the mailbox?"

"Tell them we have to know their true identities," Lisa directed.

"And we want a description of each boy," Palmer added.

"Don't you think that will sound impolite?" Amy asked.

But Shanon found a way of wording it and Amy wrote it down with her calligraphy pen.

Dear Unknown,
Thanks for your letter. Please send us your real names and some important things about you. We are four girls who live in a suite at Alma Stephens. Looking forward to your answer.

> *Yours truly,*
> *Foxes of the Third Dimension*

45

CHAPTER FIVE

"Oh, no!" groaned Palmer. "This is terrible!" She stormed into Lisa and Shanon's room, furious. In her hand was a yellow cashmere sweater. "Will you look at this ink splotch?" she whined.

"Shhh!" Lisa hissed. *"Arma virumque cano.* . . . I can't get this! Nobody speaks Latin anymore. How come we have to learn to read it out loud?"

"Because it's poetry," Shanon explained. "The rhythm is a big part of it."

"Will you two please listen to me?" Palmer insisted. "This is far more important than that stupid Latin assignment." She thrust the yellow sweater in Shanon's face.

"Too bad," Shanon murmured, taking in the black stain on the front of the sweater. "What did you do—spill ink on it?"

"Hmph!" Palmer replied. "I'd never be that careless with a sweater like this! It cost a fortune."

"Well, how did the ink get on it?" asked Lisa, peering over her Latin book.

"How do you think?" Palmer countered. "Who in this suite is always dabbling around with her fancy calligraphy pens?"

"Amy?" said Lisa.

"Correct," Palmer replied. "Our artistic little suitemate. The one I have the misfortune to be rooming with."

The door to the suite suddenly banged shut and angry footsteps came marching toward Lisa and Shanon's room. It was Amy. "Don't anybody talk to me," she warned. "I'm in a really foul mood!"

"You *are* foul," declared Palmer. "Look what you've done!" she cried, presenting her with the sweater.

"What are you complaining about now?" Amy said irritably. "And what makes you think I did something to your sweater? I never borrow your clothes." And turning on her heel, she stomped into the sitting room.

"No, of course you wouldn't borrow anything of mine," Palmer said, trailing after her. "Because I don't wear black all the time. I don't go around dressed like somebody died."

"Bug off," Amy said, glaring.

"You left your stupid calligraphy pens on top of the dresser!" Palmer was squawking. She'd followed Amy into their own bedroom.

"The top of the dresser is divided in half," Amy said. "I can't help it if you throw your clothes all over the place."

"I don't!" Palmer protested. "I'm very considerate."

"What a joke," Amy replied. "Look at the way you're hogging the whole room. Why do you need so many clothes anyway?"

"Because I'm interested in my appearance," Palmer huffed. "And that's more than I can say for you. Look at your fingernails. I never saw anything so stubby in all my life!"

"At least I don't have claws," said Amy. "Anyway, I have to keep my nails short to play the guitar." Exasperated, she plopped down on her bed and grabbed the instrument.

"And now I suppose you're going to start playing that thing. And I guess you're not even going to apologize."

Amy's eyes narrowed. "Apologize for what?"

"My sweater!" Palmer glared back at her.

Lisa crept up to their door with Shanon right behind her. "You two are getting kind of loud," Lisa suggested.

"I have to talk loud," Palmer huffed. "You can't hear yourself think over that guitar."

"That does it!" said Amy. She got up and began tugging at her bed. "I can't sleep in here."

"What's going on?" said Shanon timidly.

"I'm not staying in the same room with her another night," Amy retorted, giving the bed a big shove.

"You're going to sleep in the sitting room?" Lisa asked incredulously.

"Why not?" said Amy. "Look at what she's done to *our* room! Her stuff is everywhere. And if she's going to bug me every time I pick up my guitar—"

"I like your guitar-playing," Shanon said desperately. "I'm sure Palmer didn't really mean—"

"It's not the guitar-playing so much," Palmer put in snidely. "It's the singing. I don't know which is worse—the soppy love songs or the classical stuff."

Amy tossed the guitar onto her bed. "Forget it! I won't sing anything anymore! Just leave me alone. Anyway, you're not the only one who hates my singing."

"We like it," said Shanon.

Amy sighed. "Thanks," she said. "But unfortunately the chorus director doesn't agree with you." She turned abruptly and went back into the sitting room.

"What do you mean?" Lisa asked, coming with her. "Did something happen?"

Amy shrugged. "I was asked to leave chorus."

"What?" said Shanon. "Why? It didn't have anything to do with—"

"No, it didn't have anything to do with the ad," Amy said, smiling sadly. "I just can't read music. I told you the director only let me in because I had a low voice."

"He liked your enthusiasm, too," Lisa protested.

"That's right," Palmer chimed in, concerned in spite of herself. "And anyway, who's he going to find with a voice as low as yours?"

Amy stubbed the toe of her black shoe on the floor. "I'm sure he'll find somebody. Anyway, I've decided to go out for soccer."

"I hope that doesn't mean you're going to stop singing altogether," said Shanon. "I think your voice is . . . great."

"Yes, it's unique," said Lisa. "Totally different."

"You said it!" Palmer muttered.

Amy smiled. "Well, I'm loud—that's one thing. It's not that I ever seriously thought I could be a classical singer or anything. If they had had a rock band here at Alma. . . ."

"Exactly," Palmer chimed in. "That's the kind of music your voice is suited for."

Lisa, Shanon, and Amy all looked at her suspiciously. Why was Palmer being so nice all of a sudden?

"But I do agree that we've been getting in each other's hair in that little room," Palmer continued, ignoring their stares.

"Maybe you should keep your things more separate," Lisa suggested to Palmer. "Amy's side of the room is pretty neat. But your stuff . . . well, it does overflow some."

"Yes, it does," Palmer said helplessly. "That's why I think Amy's idea is so great."

"What idea was that?" said Amy.

"The idea that one of us should take over the sitting room. And since I've got the most stuff, it should probably be me."

"Nothing doing," said Lisa. "The sitting room's for all of us."

"You were ready to let Amy take it over," Palmer protested. "But when it comes to helping me out—"

"You and I can work this out, Palmer," Amy cut in. "We'll just have to organize things differently in our room so no one feels cramped."

"Maybe I should switch roommates," Palmer said quietly.

Amy looked hurt but was silent.

"I'm not up for change," Lisa stated.

"I'm pretty happy with things the way they are too," Shanon said.

"Oh, well, if it has to be that way," Palmer said, suddenly giving in. "I've got a stain chart buried somewhere in the bottom of one of my trunks," she said, sauntering toward the bedroom. "There's got to be a way of getting ink out of cashmere. Come move your bed back!" she called out to Amy. "It's blocking my way."

With no further argument, Amy got up and pushed the bed back into place. Shanon and Lisa went to their own room to finish studying. Soon the only sound in the suite was Lisa muttering her Latin. But then a very soft strumming came from the sitting room—Amy's guitar.

CHAPTER SIX

Shanon dashed into the *Ledger* office. "Here's the layout for the ad page. I finished it in my room last night."

Dolores was sitting at the editor's desk. Kate was scrunched up over the computer.

"Let's see," said Dolores.

"And I heard from my father," Shanon added. "He's definitely going to place a big ad for the garage."

Dolores smiled. "That certainly is generous of him!" she exclaimed. "Since none of the students here drive, they certainly don't need the services of an auto mechanic."

"Some of the girls here are old enough to drive," Shanon protested.

"Yeah, but cars aren't allowed," Kate put in. Turning, she caught Shanon's eye and looked away again.

"Well, I'm happy to get the ad," Dolores continued. *"The Ledger* can use the income. By the way," she added, handing Shanon an oversized envelope, "this came for you."

Shanon's hands trembled with excitement. The envelope was addressed to the Foxes of the Third Dimension and the return address was Kirby Hall at Ardsley. It had to be their answer from The Unknown!

"Something from Ardsley, huh?" said Dolores, eyeing Shanon curiously. "Did you actually get any pen pals?"

"Well, sort of," said Shanon. "We're not sure yet." Even though their plan was no longer a secret, the suitemates had decided to keep the details to themselves.

"Come on," Dolores urged, "why don't you open it up?"

"I can't," said Shanon. "The Foxes all have to open it together."

"Have it your way," Dolores said. "I've got to leave now anyway."

Kate and Shanon looked at each other uncomfortably as Dolores breezed out of the office. They had seen each other several times since the day Kate caught the Foxes taking the letters. But this was the first time they'd been alone together.

"I just came by to drop off the layout," said Shanon. "I can't do the typing today. We have a field trip to the arboretum."

"Is that why you're wearing those pants?" Kate couldn't help commenting. Shanon was wearing a pair of Lisa's bike pants. They were pink and green striped. Her tights, which were light green with pink hearts, were borrowed too.

"It's a bike trip," Shanon explained. "So we can wear bike pants. Mr. Griffith and Miss Grayson are going with us." She glanced down at the envelope in her hand. She could hardly wait to get back to open it.

"Before you go, there's something I have to say," Kate blurted out. "I was really stupid to report you to Miss Pryn."

"That's okay," said Shanon. "You wouldn't have thought we were a sorority if we hadn't kept things such a secret."

"When Miss Pryn called me in and told me it was just you four in the Foxes, I felt like a real idiot. I apologize."

"I apologize too," said Shanon. "We shouldn't have gone into your room. That reminds me—the picture of the boy you have on your dresser. Is his last name Giraldi?"

Kate's face flamed. "So what if it is!" she snapped. "Who have you been gossiping with? Did Dolores tell you about it—that big mouth!"

"Dolores didn't tell me anything," Shanon protested. "I was just wondering. You see, my sis—"

"Do me a favor and mind your own business," Kate cut her off. "Enough people have given me grief about Bob Giraldi."

Shanon was puzzled, but thought she'd better not ask any more questions. And at the moment she had something far more exciting to do than figuring out Kate anyway. "Sorry," she said. "I won't bring it up again." And tucking the Foxes' mail inside her down vest, she left the office and raced back to Fox Hall.

Inside the suite, Lisa, Palmer, and Amy were eating Danishes—extras they'd brought back from breakfast. In honor of the bike trip, they had all taken full advantage of the relaxed dress code. The bike pants Lisa had chosen for herself were hot pink; her bright-orange turtleneck sweater decorated with hot-pink sequins was set off by a long purple muffler wrapped several times around her neck; her dark hair was swept up on one side with a pink plastic comb. Amy had traded in her clunky shoes for some black cowboy boots with gold tips; she was wearing a black body suit and a Grateful Dead T-shirt. Palmer was dressed like a naturalist in a tweed pants suit, wide-brimmed hat, and rubber-soled oxfords; around her neck hung binoculars.

53

"Well," Palmer demanded when Shanon raced in, "any mail at *The Ledger*?" The regular responses to the pen pal ad had been dwindling. But there was only one letter they really cared about now—the answer from The Unknown.

"We got something!" Shanon said, presenting the envelope with a flourish.

"Is it from them?" Lisa gasped. "Is it from The Unknown?"

"Let's see," Amy said, rushing over.

"Bring it here!" said Palmer.

"It *is* from them!" Lisa exclaimed. "It's got to be. The return address is Kirby Hall." She grabbed the envelope.

"It's pretty big," Amy observed. "I wonder what's inside."

"There's only one way to find out," Palmer said, swiping the envelope from Lisa.

"Let Shanon open it," Lisa said. "She's the one who brought it."

Palmer grudgingly handed over the envelope. They all gathered around while Shanon opened it carefully.

"Hurry," said Lisa.

"There's more than one letter in here," Shanon said, peeking inside. "Look"—she took four smaller envelopes out of the big one—"they've each written a letter."

"Fantastic," said Lisa. "This is it. There's a letter for each of us. But each of us has to hear all four of them. Agreed?"

"I certainly want to hear all four of them," declared Palmer. "Otherwise how can I choose which one I want for a pen pal?"

"Which one *you* choose?" Lisa studied her.

"Aren't we all going to choose?" asked Shanon.

54

Amy smiled wryly. "Suppose we all want the same one?"

"I think we'd better close our eyes and each draw a letter," said Lisa, "before we open them."

"Interesting," said Amy. "Kind of like a blind date."

"I don't like blind dates," Palmer pouted. "Not that I've ever been on one."

"I think Lisa has a good idea," said Shanon.

"Oh, okay," Palmer agreed. "I'll go first."

"We'll draw to see who goes first," Lisa said. "That way everything will be done fairly."

Amy chuckled. "We're going to *draw* to *draw*?"

"Sure," said Lisa. "Why not?"

"Come on!" Palmer exploded. "Can't we just get on with it?"

Shanon tore a sheet of notepaper into four little pieces, and Amy wrote a number on each of them. Then Shanon put all the numbers in Palmer's hat and Lisa scrambled them up.

"Okay, Palmer," said Lisa. "You can draw first—*this* time."

Palmer reached into the hat and pulled out a number. "Three!" she sputtered angrily. "This is silly. My way was much better."

"Too late now," said Amy, reaching into the hat. "Ah, well," she sighed, "looks like I get last choice." She'd drawn number four.

Lisa took a deep breath and drew a number while Shanon held the hat for her. "One!" she screeched. "I go first!"

"Are you sure this wasn't fixed?" Palmer grumbled.

"Well, I guess that means I'm second," Shanon surmised, taking out the last scrap of paper.

"Let's get to the letters," said Palmer. "But if I get a boy I don't like, I'm going to trade."

"Only if someone wants to trade with you," said Lisa. "And let's decide right now that the order in which we draw the letters is also the order in which we read them out loud."

"Are you sure we shouldn't wear blindfolds?" Palmer said sarcastically.

Amy giggled. "This is getting deep."

"Well, we *are* Foxes of the Third Dimension," Shanon piped up, laughing.

"We need something bigger than a hat to put the letters in," Amy said, turning businesslike.

They put the letters in Lisa's book bag, shook them up, and then opened the bag just wide enough for one person to get a hand in.

"Okay, Lisa," Amy said, holding the bag.

Lisa giggled. "I hope nothing bites me."

"And don't open it up yet!" said Palmer. "Wait until everybody has one."

"Agreed," said Lisa. She pulled out a long white envelope with no writing on the outside of it. Shanon stepped up and drew one just like Lisa's. Then it was Palmer's turn. Her envelope was also the same size and white with no writing on it.

"Well," said Amy, reaching in for the remaining letter. "I'm sure we all know what mine will look like."

The four Foxes started laughing. They were each holding identical envelopes with nothing on the outside.

"These Unknowns must be fun guys," said Lisa.

Palmer rolled her eyes. "They definitely planned this."

"They want to be mysterious," said Amy, "just like us."

"Suppose there's nothing inside but blank paper." Shanon giggled.

They sat down in a circle. "I don't think so," said Lisa, tearing open the first envelope. The message was scrawled on notebook paper with big black letters. "Look at this!" she screeched. "It's incredible!"

Hey, Fox of the Third Dimension,
My name is Robert Williams, but you can call me Robby. All I can say about my looks is: no ninety-pound weakling!
P.S. I've appeared as a centerfold.

"A centerfold?" Shanon gasped. "He's a model in a magazine?"

"He probably lifts weights," said Palmer.

"Maybe he's a hulk," said Amy.

"A hulk?" said Lisa. "I hope you mean a hunk. Anyway, he's got to be tall, if he's 'no ninety-pound weakling.' Listen, there's another P.S."

P.P.S. Naturally, we'd like to know your true identities also. Since there are four of us and four of you, I suppose each Unknown gets one Fox for a pen pal. Please have my pen pal write me right away telling her deepest dreams and desires along with some vital statistics.

Amy's mouth dropped open. "Vital statistics?"

"I wonder what he's talking about," drawled Palmer with a smile.

"He can't be asking for your . . ." Shanon's voice trailed off.

"My measurements?" Lisa laughed loudly. "I'll tell him how tall I am."

"You'd better hope he's six feet then," said Palmer.

Amy laughed. "If he's too short, you can trade with me."

"Vital statistics!" Lisa echoed the phrase indignantly. "This guy's got nerve, anyway."

"I think we should decide right now not to tell them anything but our height," said Palmer. "Anything else is just too personal."

"What's the matter?" Amy said slyly. Palmer wore bras but she always stuffed them. "You sound like someone with something to hide."

"Very funny," said Palmer.

Shanon giggled. "What about your dreams and desires, Lisa? Are you going to write them?"

Lisa smiled. "I'll think of something." And turning to Shanon, she said, "Go ahead. Read yours now."

Shanon opened her envelope and quickly glanced at the note. "You won't believe the name of this guy," she said, shaking her head in disbelief. "And the description. . . ."

"Read it!" said Lisa.

Dear Fox of the Third Dimension,

Since you want to know, my name is Mars. If you need a description, here it is: I'M A GOD!

P.S. Please send your own description.

"Awesome," said Lisa, snatching the letter out of Shanon's hands.

"Sounds a little conceited, if you ask me," Shanon laughed.

"Well, Mars was an ancient Roman god, wasn't he?" said Palmer. "He's just doing a takeoff on his name. I wonder what a guy with a name like Mars could look like?"

"Like an ancient Roman," Amy said.

"Or something from outer space!" Lisa suggested.

"He wants a description of me too," Shanon said, taking the letter back. "If he's supposed to be a god, what am I going to write? He probably—"

"You can figure it out later," Palmer broke in. "I'm going to open mine now!"

The handwriting in the letter that Palmer pulled out of her white envelope was extremely neat and small.

Dear Fox of the Third Dimension,

I think your idea to be pen pals is delightful. My name is John Adams and I guess the best way to describe myself is to say that I'm a poet and a jock. I do think we'd be better off in coeducational schools even at our age, but I guess the coaches wouldn't like it, because we guys would always be breaking our training. At this point, the thought of talking to a girl about anything sounds great, especially in a letter. Hope to hear from you soon.

P.S. Naturally, I want to know something about my particular pen pal.

Palmer tossed the letter onto the bed. "Nothing too exciting there."

"What's wrong with it?" said Amy.

"He sounds like a boring person," said Palmer. "And look at his handwriting. It's so perfect-looking."

"Let's see mine," said Amy. She tore open the fourth letter. It was on thick white stationery, but was full of smudges and erasures.

Dear Fox,
My name is Simmie Randolph the Third. I am indescribable.

"He had trouble spelling 'indescribable,'" Lisa said, looking over Amy's shoulder. "Look how many times he erased it."

"I like the name Simmie," said Amy.

"Indescribable," muttered Shanon. "That's almost as bad as saying you're a god."

"I think it's cute," disagreed Palmer. "I'll take him."

"But I drew his letter," said Amy. "I thought that was the idea—to draw your pen pal."

"I still don't like that idea," said Palmer. "John Adams sounds really dull."

"You can't be sure of that from just one letter, can you?" said Shanon.

"We agreed that the letter we drew would be our pen pal," Lisa said emphatically. "You'll just have to give John Adams a chance, Palmer."

"No," said Palmer, "we said we could trade. And I want to trade for Simmie Randolph."

"That's up to Amy," said Lisa.

Amy looked at Palmer. "Sorry," she said flatly. "I don't want to."

60

"Why not?" Palmer exclaimed. "We don't even know who these boys are yet."

Amy shrugged. "Yeah, that's why I don't think there's any point in trading. I think it's sort of fun to go with the 'unknown.' "

"Cute," laughed Lisa. "The unknown!" She turned to Palmer. "Relax—this is only for fun, remember? John Adams is probably a very interesting person."

"That's right," said Shanon. "He writes poetry."

There was a light knock on the door, and Lisa went to open it. There stood Miss Grayson dressed in jeans and looking uncharacteristically stern. "The group is waiting for you downstairs, girls," she told them.

Flushed, Shanon got up and almost tripped. "Sorry, Miss Grayson," she said. "We were just. . . ."

"We got some letters in the mail," volunteered Lisa.

Miss Grayson's violet eyes twinkled, but she still wasn't smiling. "Yes, I heard that this suite's the home of the mysterious Foxes."

"I guess we should have told you," Lisa said humbly.

"Yes, I think you should have," Miss Grayson said. "As you know, I never objected to your ad. The idea seems like fun. But"—she cast her eyes toward Palmer—"I hope you'll be more honest in the future. I'm here to help you, and I don't appreciate being lied to."

Shanon, Amy, and Lisa nodded mutely and Palmer looked away.

"Now, let's go!" said Miss Grayson. "It's a beautiful day and we're going on a bike trip! This is no time for long faces."

The Foxes grabbed their packs and jackets and bounded down the stairway. Outside, the rest of the group was waiting. Mr. Griffith was dressed in jeans and a red wool shirt that made him look like a lumberjack.

"Come on, girls!" he called in his deep voice. And turning to Miss Grayson, he smiled and said, "Want to take the front or the back of the group, Maggie?"

Miss Grayson blushed. "I'll take the lead if you don't mind, Dan."

Lisa nudged Amy. "Did you hear that?" she whispered. "He called her Maggie."

"Dan," Palmer sighed. "That must be short for Daniel."

The weather was crisp and the ride to the arboretum pleasant. "It really looks like fall now," Shanon said, pedaling along beside Lisa.

Lisa nodded in agreement. "The leaves are turning. I think I'll collect some and make notecards in the art studio for my grandmother."

"Notecards out of leaves?" said Shanon.

"You press a leaf and seal it in plastic," Lisa explained. "It makes a pretty cover. I made some last year and Gammy really liked them."

The girls shifted gears to take a hill. Up ahead was Miss Grayson, and a little behind with Mr. Griffith and the rest of the group were Amy and Palmer.

"Do you really think it's okay to write to these guys?" Shanon asked suddenly. "I mean, we don't exactly know them."

"What harm can it do?" grunted Lisa. "I know what you mean, though—they might be total drips. But there's one way I can find out for us."

"How?" asked Shanon.

Lisa gave her a look at the top of the hill. "I have a brother over at Ardsley, remember?"

Getting Reggie on the telephone that night wasn't easy. First, the girls had to take turns standing in line for the pay phone. Then the phone on Reggie's floor at Ardsley was busy, and then some boy said he was going to try to find him and left Lisa on hold. Finally, after five minutes and some whining from one of the second-floor girls who wanted to make a call too, Reggie picked up the phone.

"What does Robby Williams look like?" Lisa asked, as soon as she'd said "Hello" and "How are you?"

"He's okay," answered Reggie.

"How about John Adams?"

"Okay too," Reggie replied.

Lisa got a little impatient. "Is that all you can say, Reggie—just okay?"

There was a silence on the phone. "He's not saying anything!" whispered Lisa to the others. "Come on, Reg," she wheedled, "this is important."

"Why are you so interested in these guys?" he wanted to know.

"I'm asking for a friend," Lisa said, thinking fast. She didn't think her brother would like knowing she was one of the Foxes. And she was sure her mother would object too. "Please, Reggie," she prodded. "Can't you tell me something?"

"Ask him about Simmie Randolph!" nudged Amy.

Lisa asked.

"Simmie Randolph I think I saw once," Reggie replied. "He has blond hair, right? He looks like an actor."

Lisa put her hand over the receiver. "He knows Simmie!" she gasped. "He's blond and really good-looking!"

Amy smiled brightly.

63

Shanon moved in. "Ask about Mars."

Lisa asked.

Reggie laughed. "Mars, you say? I never heard of him. What is he—an alien?"

Realizing that she wouldn't get any more information, Lisa said good-bye and hung up. "Sorry," she told her suitemates. "My brother can be a real pain sometimes."

"Maybe he should hook up with Kate Majors," Palmer said wryly.

"At least we know Simmie has blond hair," Amy said as the group started off down the corridor.

"Well, what are we going to do now?" Shanon asked once they were back in the suite behind closed doors.

"Let's just write and see what they write back," replied Lisa.

CHAPTER SEVEN

Dear Robby,

    Guess you're wondering about the Foxes' real names. So I'll tell you. My name is Lisa McGreevy and I actually have a brother who goes to Ardsley and he says you are okay. You may not know him. His name is Reggie McGreevy and he is a computer genius. He is in fifth form. Anyway, this letter is supposed to be about me, right? Ha ha! I am tall for my age—5'6". Guess you are tall too, from your description. My dream is to go to Europe by myself and maybe to Alaska. I don't dream much at night, but once I had this nightmare about a whale. It was horrible!! My desire is to do well at Alma so my mother will let me out to go to art school. My favorite subject is French, even though I have to work on my accent.

    Do you take French? And also, are you a real model? In what magazine? Hope we enjoy writing to each other.

Yours truly,
Lisa McGreevy

Dear Simmie,

My name is Amy Ho and I am Chinese-American, but my family has lived all over the world because of my dad's business.

My favorite artists are Cyndi Lauper and Joan Jett. One day I would like to be a recording artist too. I think it is high art to stand in front of people and not be afraid to make incredible sounds like that. My father ignores this and expects me to be a scientist, which I probably will not become. I don't like science except for biology. We are dissecting frogs this term and I can't wait. (Hope this isn't a gross-out.) I do like math, though, and it is my best subject. I have advanced standing in math here. Anyway, there's not much danger of my becoming a recording artist because I'm not a great singer. My roommate will tell you that much. But some people say you don't have to sing that well—that a lot is personality on stage.

My favorite color is black. My hobbies are jogging, ice-skating, and calligraphy. I have just made the soccer team! I'm happy you'll be my pen pal.

Yours truly,
Amy

Dear John,

Look forward to writing you although I'm afraid I don't like poetry. But maybe I'll like some of yours.

Sincerely,
Palmer Durand

Dear Mars,

I have never heard of a name

Dear Mars,
My name is Shanon Davis and I

Hi, Mars,
Greetings from the planet Earth . . .

"All you have to do is say something about yourself," said Lisa.

Shanon bit her pencil.

"Anything!" said Lisa. "You're a writer! You work for the newspaper."

"That's different," Shanon said, studying the clean sheet of paper before her.

Lisa sat down on the bed beside her. "Please, Shanon. It's been four days since The Unknowns wrote to us, and everybody's finished her letter but you."

"It's not that easy to describe yourself in a letter," Shanon said irritably. Suddenly she felt uncomfortable in Lisa's borrowed rugby shirt. Suddenly she felt uncomfortable about the whole thing. "Maybe you should just send your letters without mine."

"Nothing doing!" Lisa exclaimed. "We're in this together. I thought you thought having a pen pal would be fun."

"I do think it's fun," said Shanon. "It's just harder than I expected."

"But you were the one who wrote all those notes to Arthur Stuart," argued Lisa.

Shanon sighed. "That was different. I knew Arthur all the way from first grade. This boy Mars is a total stranger. Anyway," she added, "why would a boy who says he's a god be interested in me?"

Lisa laughed. "So that's what's bothering you! He's not a god—he's just a regular boy. He was only goofing around."

"I know that," said Shanon. "I'm not stupid. It's just that I want my first letter to be interesting, and I don't know how to describe myself."

"Just tell him what you look like," Lisa suggested.

"I'm not doing that!" Shanon said. "Are you kidding?"

"Why not?" asked Lisa.

Shanon shrugged. "Why do you think? When it comes to my looks, there's nothing special."

"That's not true!" said Lisa. "Your hair is beautiful—it's so thick. And your eyes . . ."

Shanon shook her head. "I'm okay, I guess. But take a look at Doreen." She pointed to the picture of her sister she kept on her dresser. Doreen Davis had long, wavy blond hair, impish blue eyes, and dimples. Her skin and teeth looked perfect. "When you've got somebody like that in the house, it's hard not to have an inferiority complex."

"Your sister *is* beautiful," Lisa agreed, "but so are you."

Shanon smiled. "You think so?"

Lisa put an arm around her shoulder. "Sure I do. Now, go write your letter."

"I'm still stuck," said Shanon. "Maybe I should start off with my deepest dreams and desires. That's what Rob asked you."

"Good idea!" Lisa encouraged.

Shanon thought for a minute. "That's no good either. The only dreams I remember having are about Arthur Stuart. I'm sure Mars wouldn't want to hear about those."

Lisa sighed. "I guess not. But dreams can also mean ambitions—what you'd like to do."

68

"That's easy," said Shanon. "I've had the same ambition almost my whole life."

"I can guess what that is," said Lisa. "To be a writer."

Shanon smiled. "Nope. I like to write. But my real dream is to be . . . an astronaut."

Lisa smiled softly. "That's a wonderful dream."

"Well, it's only a dream," said Shanon. "I wouldn't even know how to go about doing something like that."

Lisa rolled over onto the bed. "You and I are really different," she·mused. "If I had this dream of being an astronaut when I grew up I'd think it was so cool, I'd blab it all over the place. But you keep it to yourself."

"I guess I am the quiet type," said Shanon.

"This thing about becoming an astronaut is really neat," said Lisa. "I bet Mars would think it's interesting."

Shanon giggled. "Yeah, especially since his name is the name of a planet."

Lisa playfully tossed her a pillow. "So, come on—write your letter."

Shanon bit the tip of her pencil. "Okay. I guess I can think of something."

Lisa sat up suddenly. "I know! There's a game I used to play with my friend at home. It may help you!"

"What do I have to do?"

"Just close your eyes and blurt out the first thing that comes into your mind," Lisa instructed. "I'm going to ask you some questions."

Shanon flopped back onto the bed. "Fire away."

"If you, Shanon Davis, were a flower," she asked, "what flower would you be?"

"A petunia," said Shanon with no hesitation.

Lisa smiled. "What if you were a piece of music?"

Shanon giggled. " 'The Star-Spangled Banner'!"

Lisa smiled. "And what color would you be?"

"Yellow."

"I think you're right," said Lisa. "Yellow is also the color of the sun, and from the start I thought you were a pretty warm person."

Shanon opened her eyes. "Really?"

"Uh-huh."

"If you were a color, you'd probably be red," Shanon told Lisa. "You're really out there."

"Amy would definitely be black," Lisa said, "don't you think?"

"No, she'd probably be deep green, like an ocean with lots of stuff going on underneath," said Shanon. "Black's just her favorite color. I like this game. It's interesting. What about Palmer?"

Lisa shrugged. "What about her?"

Shanon thought. "If Palmer were a body of water, what would she be?"

"A drip," said Lisa wickedly.

"You really don't like her much, do you?"

"She's okay," Lisa answered. "I just don't like the way she treats Amy. She can be pretty insensitive."

Shanon sat up and started writing.

"What are you doing?" asked Lisa. "Are you going to write Mars?"

"Sure. It shouldn't take long. I guess I was taking the whole thing too seriously."

"I should take math that seriously," Lisa said. "I haven't got the brain for it, like Amy. Actually, maybe I should write to Gammy now. I wish I would hear from Mom or

Dad, but I think they're in the Caribbean on some kind of business trip."

Shanon reached out and touched her roommate's elbow. "Hey, Lisa . . ."

"What?"

"Thanks."

After Shanon finished her letter to Mars, she showed it to Lisa.

Dear Mars,

I am not a celestial being like you are. Actually, I am probably what you call ordinary. I like to read a lot and I grew up just a few miles from here. I am a good biker, and at home I used to make brownies. I have a great big family. Both sets of my grandparents live with us. And I have a big sister and three little brothers. My ambition is to be a writer someday. (But my secret ambition is to be an astronaut.) I spend a lot of time working for the school newspaper. I look forward to getting to know you through our letters.

Yours truly,
Shanon Davis

P.S. If I were a flower I'd be a petunia, and if I were a piece of music I'd be 'The Star-Spangled Banner.' Isn't that a riot? Write soon.

CHAPTER EIGHT

Dear Lisa,

First of all, I guess I should be straight with you. I was just fooling around when I said I was in a centerfold. Actually, I did once appear in a newspaper. I was in Alaska one summer and I rescued this family from a flood because there was nobody around to drive the truck but me. Guess you're surprised that I know how to drive. My grandfather taught me when I was eleven. He has a farm and he let me drive his tractor. Anyway, the guy I was working for had gone off and left his wife and baby and it was going to be hard for his wife to drive because she had just come home from the hospital from having the new baby. So she trusted me to do it. And I did even though I was scared because the water was really rising. That's how I got my picture in the paper. Maybe this is not interesting to you. I don't know.

Signing off for now,
Robert Williams

P.S. I am 5'9" and still growing. Please send a picture of yourself in your next letter.

Dear Amy,

    I thought your letter was amuzing. I have traveled a lot but never lived anywhere but Palm Beach. Where else have you lived? Do you speak Chinese?

Love,
Simmie

P.S. Please send picture.

Dear Palmer,

    Here is something I wrote a while back:

> This arch age
> Over the mushroom sky
> Roars with muzzled discontent
> Tricked by rates of percentage
> Until we are mortgaged
> Ragged souls, sons of
> Energy Wasted, spilled in the
> Deep Ocean, but not deep enough

    I tried to get this in the literary magazine here at Ardsley, but it was turned down. But that doesn't depress me. The types who run the mag are questionable in my book. I like to play tennis. Do you play? Please send a picture.

Yours truly,
John Adams

Dear Shanon Davis,

    Your name has an earthly ring to it that I like. Mind sending me a picture?

From Mars

Even though it was only twenty minutes to curfew, the girls ran across the quad for something to eat. Lisa had found out how simple it was to raid the kitchen a few days back, and ever since they'd been having snacks there. Tonight the letters had made them super hungry, especially the part about The Unknowns wanting pictures.

"What do you think?" said Palmer. "Should we send them our pictures?"

"Definitely," Lisa answered, pulling out a box of chocolate doughnuts and some juice.

"I don't know if I want to," said Shanon. "I mean, I haven't even got a decent snapshot."

"Neither have I," said Amy. She opened a bag of chocolate chips and passed them to Shanon.

"Where did these come from?" Shanon muttered.

"Mrs. Butter probably keeps them for baking," said Amy, munching.

Shanon reached in and took a handful. It had been so long since she'd tasted chocolate and her face was really clear these days.

Lisa passed around the doughnuts, which were thick with fudgy icing. "I don't have a picture of myself either, but that's no problem. We'll just take new ones."

"How?" Amy asked. "Do you have a camera?"

Lisa shook her head.

"That's a problem," said Palmer. "I don't have one either. But anyway, maybe we shouldn't send pictures."

Shanon nervously nibbled a handful of chocolate chips. "How come?"

"Because we're the ones who are supposed to be deciding if we want to write to them!" Palmer said hotly. "And now they want *our* pictures."

74

"But we've already decided to write them," Lisa said, smiling. "And they've decided to write us. It's only natural that they'd want to know what we look like."

"Hmph!" said Palmer. "I want to know what they look like too. I hope John Adams looks better than his poetry sounds."

"I liked his poem," Amy said. "Did you notice it's an acrostic?"

Palmer looked puzzled.

"The first letter of each line spells out a word," Amy explained.

"What word?" asked Lisa.

Amy smiled wryly. *Tortured!*

Palmer rolled her eyes. "Depressing. What's there to be tortured about? The poem made absolutely no sense to me."

"We'd better get out of here," Shanon reminded them. "It's getting late."

"You're right," said Lisa, wiping their crumbs off the counter. "Let's put this stuff away."

"The chocolate chips are all gone," said Shanon sheepishly. "I guess I ate too many."

Lisa turned out the light at the door. "Forget about food. What we need now is a camera!"

"Maybe I can get one from the newspaper," said Shanon as they crossed the quad to the dorm. "I've seen a few cameras there—including a Polaroid! We wouldn't even have to wait to get the film developed."

"What happens if we send pictures to The Unknown and they don't like them?" asked Amy.

"Why wouldn't they?" said Palmer.

"I don't know," said Amy. "To some boys, looks mean a lot."

75

"But all of us are really attractive," Lisa argued. She glanced at Shanon. "Right?"

"Sure," gulped Shanon. "But I know what Amy means. We may not look like the ideal girls to them."

Palmer sniffed. "Who cares? John Adams isn't exactly my ideal poet, either."

. "In any case," said Lisa, "looks aren't everything." She held open the outside door for them.

"Yes, they are," Palmer disagreed, leading the way to the staircase. "I mean, look at Kate Majors."

"What about her?" said Shanon.

They walked into 3-D and stopped in the sitting room. "Kate is mousy," said Palmer. "And that's why she's probably never had a boyfriend."

"I think she *has* had a boyfriend," said Lisa.

"Hey, that's right," said Shanon. "Dolores told me that some boy once broke Kate's heart or something."

"I wonder who he was?" Amy said curiously.

"I think it was a guy named Bob Giraldi," said Shanon, hanging up Lisa's bright-blue poncho. "I saw his picture on Kate's dresser, and she got real mad when I asked her about him. She'd be even madder if she knew that Bob Giraldi was the boy from Ardsley my sister used to date."

"No kidding!" said Lisa. "That's juicy."

Shanon sighed. "I remember Doreen said there was some younger girl at Alma who had a crush on Bob. I bet it was Kate."

"Heavy," said Amy.

"Well, now we have something on Kate, anyway," Palmer chortled.

Shanon looked alarmed. "Don't you dare breathe a word about this. It might embarrass Kate."

"I guess you're right," said Palmer. "Anyway, we don't

76

want to get on her bad side again. She's so eager to report people."

"I feel sorry for Kate," said Amy. "It sounds like she got dumped."

"I think she must have been," said Shanon. "Think how one of us would feel if that happened to us."

"Why worry about Kate," Palmer said irritably. "Let's concentrate on our own problems."

"Okay," agreed Lisa. "How about the camera, Shanon? Do you think you can get it?"

Shanon nodded. "I'll try."

The next morning when Shanon went to the newspaper office, Dolores wasn't there yet, but Kate was already at her desk.

"We've got some transcribing for you to do today, Shanon," Kate said, sounding very assistant-editorish. "Dolores did an interview with Mr. Griffith. The tape is on the dictaphone."

"You mean I get to listen to Mr. Griffith's deep voice?" Shanon giggled uncomfortably. "By the way, I like your vest."

Kate looked Shanon over. "I like your socks," she replied shortly.

The anklet socks that Shanon was wearing were purple with little orange sequins around the cuff. "Neat, huh? They're Lisa's. She sewed the sequins on herself."

"Don't you ever wear any of your own clothes?" Kate asked.

"Sure . . ." Shanon replied. She was about to explain that her own clothes were too boring, but stopped herself. After all, Kate had the same kind of wardrobe.

Kate took her glasses off and stared at Shanon for a

moment, her pale gray eyes looking surprisingly warm. "I'm sorry I yelled at you the other day," she finally said. "It's just that the picture of that certain person, er, Bob, that you happened to see . . . well, it brings up some unpleasant memories."

"I'm sorry," Shanon said. She wanted to tell Kate about the coincidence with Doreen dating Bob too, but she was afraid that would only make things worse.

"What's the newspaper's policy on the Polaroid camera?" Shanon said instead.

Kate put her glasses back on. "It's for official newspaper business only."

"Official newspaper business, huh?" Shanon thought hard, trying to figure out some way that taking the Foxes' pictures could be good for the newspaper. "It's not exactly official business," she admitted, "but I would like to borrow the camera. I'd be really careful. Actually, it's for—"

"For your pen pals?" asked Kate, lifting an eyebrow.

"Well, yes," said Shanon. "I guess it sounds pretty silly. But the boys want pictures and we don't have any."

Kate thought for a minute. "Okay. After all, you're not asking to use the thirty-five millimeter. But I'd better be the one who uses the camera. Dolores is very possessive about the equipment."

"You mean you'll take our pictures?" Shanon asked, surprised.

Kate nodded. "I still owe you one for that mess I got you into with Miss Pryn."

"Thanks," said Shanon. "How soon can we do it?"

Kate smiled. "Tomorrow."

CHAPTER NINE

Dear Robert,

(I thought you like to be called Robby, but you signed your name Robert. Which one do you like better?)

Yes, I found your adventure in Alaska with the flood very exciting. My suitemates couldn't believe it when I told them!!! Anyway, nothing that exciting ever happened to me except the time when my brother Reggie forgot me at the school I used to go to. Reggie forgets a lot of things. So I tried to walk home by myself. (This was back in Pennsylvania where I come from.) Anyway, I got lost and this lady found me and took me to a circus. She worked there selling programs or something. And I got to see the circus people close up. My mother couldn't understand why the lady didn't bring me right home, but I think she didn't want to be late for work. Luckily, I remembered my phone number. Don't you think it is ridiculous that we don't have phones at Alma and Ardsley? In our own rooms, that is? More than anything I would like to have a phone in my room. Then I would talk to people.

See ya (I mean write ya!),
Lisa
P.S. Please send a photograph of yourself.

Dear Simmie,

You asked where we had lived. Besides New York City, I guess my longest time in another place was Sydney, Australia. My best friend from when I was little still lives there. Her name is Evon. I also lived in England and Thailand when I was a baby, but most of my grammar school days were in New York.

I don't speak Chinese, but I can write some of the characters. My mom and dad speak the language to each other and so does my grandmother. My grandmother also serves me these neat breakfasts with bacon, eggs, and rice instead of bacon, eggs, and Rice Krispies. Maybe someday you'll meet my family. Maybe someday you'll meet me.

Thank you for saying that my letter was amazing.

Send a picture.

Sincerely,
Amy

Dear John,

It was hard to understand your poem. Amusing however that it was an acrostic for TORTURED. I got that right away. I hope this doesn't hurt your feelings. Since you asked for a picture of me, I would also like a picture of you.

Yours truly,
Palmer Durand

Dear Mars,

What are your favorite subjects at school? I would like to find out more about you. Is the food good at Ardsley?

It's really good here. We have this cook named Mrs. Worth and everybody calls her Mrs. Butter (like in Mrs. Butterworth's syrup—cute, huh?). Please write soon and I hope you won't mind sending a picture.

Sincerely,
Shanon

P.S. What did you mean when you called me earthly?

The letters were out in the sitting room, ready for the mailbox. The girls had written them the night before. Only the pictures were missing.

"How do I look?" Lisa asked brightly.

"Great," Shanon mumbled, half asleep. "What time is it?"

"Seven. Kate's going to be here in half an hour."

Shanon jumped out of bed. "Wow! I'd better get dressed."

"I think this red turtleneck is a good choice, don't you?" Lisa asked, adjusting her sweater. "Look—I've got my grandfather's gold watch around my neck! Gammy gave it to me for my last birthday."

Shanon looked in the mirror and groaned. "Oh, no!"

"What is it?" Lisa asked, coming over.

Shanon turned around. "Look at me!" she cried. "Look at my chin—I've got a pimple!"

"Wow," Lisa murmured.

"It must be all that chocolate I ate the other night," Shanon moaned miserably.

"Don't worry," Lisa said. "You can cover it up with makeup."

"Morning, everybody!"

"Morning, Amy," said Lisa and Shanon. Amy was already dressed.

"I love your earrings!" exclaimed Lisa.

"Thanks," said Amy. "I thought I'd wear something different for the photos." As usual, Amy was all in black—this time it was a jumpsuit that made her look like a pilot. But in her ears were two outrageously long gold spirals. Grabbing Lisa's mousse from the dresser, she rubbed it through her hair. "What's wrong with you?" she asked, looking at Shanon.

"Nothing but the biggest pimple in the world," Shanon replied, heading for the closet.

"Oh, yeah," said Amy. "Are you sure it's a pimple? It looks more like a bite to me."

"Hi there, you all!" Palmer waltzed in wearing a lacy pale-blue dress that matched her eyes perfectly.

"What are you doing in a party dress?" said Lisa. "We all agreed to wear something casual."

"I changed my mind," said Palmer nonchalantly. She was wearing high-heeled pumps and stockings and loads of pink lipstick. "If this guy writes poetry, I want to look poetic. Anyway, I'm not really a casual kind of person."

"Leave it to my roommate to change things in midstream," said Amy.

"Can I help it if I have a mind of my own?" Palmer said. "Anyway, how do I look?"

"Great," Lisa said flatly. "As if you're going to a prom or something. I just hope you don't show the rest of us up."

Palmer smiled smugly. "Don't worry, I won't. You all look adorable." She looked at Shanon, who was holding a pink cotton dress. "Is *that* what you're going to wear? I wouldn't. Pink isn't your color."

"But it's the only dress I ironed," Shanon said miserably. She held the dress up to the mirror. "Maybe you're right. If I wear something brighter, it might distract from my face."

"What's wrong with your face?" Palmer said, studying Shanon's pimple. "Is that a mosquito bite or acne?"

"I give up!" Shanon wailed. "Can't we just forget this whole thing?"

"Wait a minute," Lisa said, marching over. "This pink dress is perfectly fine. Unless you want to borrow something from me."

"This is my best dress," said Shanon. "For once I thought I'd wear my own clothes."

"The pink dress looks great on you," said Amy. "Wear it. Only you'd better hurry up. Kate will be here any minute now."

Shanon hurriedly pulled on the dress, then tried to cover the pimple with Lisa's makeup. But there was no way to disguise the blemish. "I look ridiculous," she said.

"No, you don't," Lisa said, trying to be encouraging.

"Don't worry about it," Palmer said. "You're not the only teen in the world with a skin problem."

There was a knock on the sitting-room door.

"Here I am," Kate announced, coming in with the camera.

"It's really nice of you to help us out," said Lisa. "Why don't we do it in the sitting room? The loveseat is a nice place, don't you think?"

"Fine," Kate said.

Shanon forced a smile. At least her pink dress matched the loveseat.

"Okay," said Kate. "Who's first? What about you, Shanon?"

Shanon tugged at her dress and pushed her hair back. "Ready as I'll ever be."

"What's that splotch on your face?" asked Kate. "Are you allergic to something?"

"It's a pimple," gulped Shanon. "I hope it won't come out in the picture."

Kate took two snapshots of Shanon and two of each of the other girls.

"Wait," said Lisa. "Let's take one together."

"All right," said Kate good-naturedly. The four Foxes stood in front of the loveseat and Kate snapped their picture. Then they all gathered around to see the results.

"Wow!" said Lisa, seeing their figures emerge in the photograph. "That's sensational!"

Shanon, Amy, and Palmer sat down on the loveseat to go over their own individual snapshots.

"These are awful," Shanon said. "The pimple shows in both of them."

Lisa came over to look. "I don't think it's so bad. Except for the blemish, your face looks great. In fact, you look a lot like that picture of your sister."

"I could never look like Doreen," Shanon exclaimed. "She's too beautiful."

"No, Lisa's right," said Amy excitedly. She skipped into Lisa and Shanon's room and came back with the framed snapshot. "You look a lot like her here."

Kate came closer. "Who's that?" she asked.

"Doreen Davis," Palmer announced. "Shanon's sister. Isn't she drop-dead gorgeous?"

Shanon gulped and sank down into the loveseat. Amy hung her head, and Lisa jabbed Palmer with her elbow, while Kate stood there glaring.

"Yes, she's gorgeous all right," Kate said through clenched teeth. She looked at Shanon. "Is your sister Doreen Davis the same Doreen Davis who lives in Brighton and went to the public high school and . . . who used to date Bob Giraldi?"

Shanon swallowed. "Yes, that's her."

Kate's mouth quivered angrily. "Thanks for telling me, Shanon! Thanks a lot!" She stormed out, taking the camera.

"At least she left us the pictures," Palmer said. "I think mine turned out really good."

"Why did you do that?" Shanon accused her. "Kate's feelings must really be hurt, and now she's mad at me!"

"Yeah," Amy breathed, "that was low, Palmer."

"What do you mean?" Palmer said innocently. "I didn't tell her on purpose. Anyway, Lisa and Amy were the ones who brought Doreen up in the first place."

"You're right," Lisa said humbly. "I'm sorry, Shanon."

Shanon sighed. "I guess Kate would have found out sooner or later anyway."

"It's not as if this guy took *you* out," said Palmer. "It was your sister. Anyway, Kate will get over it."

"I hope so," said Shanon. "It was really nice of her to take these pictures."

"Yeah, they're good," said Amy. "Let's put them in the envelopes right now."

"I don't know which one of mine to send," said Palmer. "They both look so good."

As Lisa, Palmer, and Amy went about putting their snapshots in the envelopes, Shanon hung back on the loveseat agonizing. "Which one are you going to use?" Lisa asked her.

85

"I . . . haven't decided yet," Shanon hedged.

"Well, choose," said Lisa. "We might as well mail them. I'm going past Booth Hall on my way to the language lab."

"I'll be passing Booth myself in a little while," Shanon volunteered. "On my way to the library. I can put all four letters in the mailbox then."

"Thanks," said Lisa, grabbing her poncho.

"Wait up," said Amy. "I'll walk with you. I've got to go to the gym to talk with the soccer coach."

It took Palmer a lot more than a minute to change into her cashmere sweater and tweed skirt, but finally the three girls left the suite and Shanon was alone with the letters. Hers was the only one that hadn't been sealed yet. As she looked at the pictures of herself that Kate had taken, her eyes welled up with tears of frustration. The pimple on her chin really stood out—it was horrible!

As Shanon threw herself down on the loveseat, her eye fell on the picture of Doreen. It was lying right next to her. "I wish I had something like this," Shanon sighed, slipping the snapshot out of the frame for a closer look.

Suddenly she thought, Why not send this one! Who would know the difference? By the time she and Mars met—if they ever did . . . No! She couldn't do that. It would be dishonest. But how could she send Mars a terrible picture of herself?

And then, before she could talk herself out of it, Shanon opened her letter to Mars and added a snapshot. But it wasn't one of her own photos—it was her sister Doreen's.

CHAPTER TEN

Dear Lisa,

I got your picture and I really liked it. I like turtlenecks, especially red ones. Is that necklace you're wearing some kind of medal or is it a pocket watch? I'm glad you were interested in my time in Alaska. I forgot to say that I was working on a wildlife project that summer. I was on a farm taking care of some musk-ox. Every summer my dad sends me away somewhere. I hope one time it will be to Europe. Maybe you'll go the same year and we'll bump into each other.

Signing off for now,
Rob

Dear Amy,

Your haircut is rad. Also, those are some amuzing earrings. I hope to meet you someday in person.

Love,
Simmie Randolph

Dear Palmer,

I'm sorry you didn't like my poem. But that's okay.

Everybody can't have the same taste. Maybe sometime I can show you some more of my stuff and there will be something that you do like. Poetry is not the only thing I'm interested in. As I told you, I'm also a jock. I just got word that I made the football team and I'm in training. Yaah! I think physical fitness is very important, don't you? My dad still works out even though he's almost forty. He says that if there's ever a national emergency, he wants to be able to run away from it. He doesn't want to rely on an automobile to get out of the city. And I must say I agree with him. Please tell me some more about yourself.

Sincerely,
John

P.S. Your picture is beautiful.

Dear Shanon,
    YOU ARE A GODDESS!

Mars

"Mr. Griffith's eyes were definitely green today," said Amy, coming out of English.

"Definitely," sighed Shanon. "In fact this whole day is kind of greenish, if you ask me." She looked across the quadrangle. "Really emerald."

"What are you two talking about?" Palmer asked, coming up behind with Lisa.

"Nothing really," Amy said. "It's just such a beautiful day!"

"It is," Lisa agreed. And turning to Shanon, she said, "Nice paper."

Shanon smiled. "Thanks. I was really surprised when Mr. Griffith asked me to read it in class."

"I wasn't," said Amy. "After all, you got an A!"

"As usual," groaned Palmer. "I don't know what you and I do differently, but I can't seem to get anything but C's in any subject."

"That's because you don't like studying," Amy told her.

"Yes, I do," she protested. "Studying's just not my favorite thing, that's all."

"Let's go get apples!" said Lisa. "Race you to the tree!" She sprinted ahead with Amy, leaving Shanon and Palmer to catch up. They cut around Booth Hall to the gymnasium. The apple tree was on a hill near the track, overlooking the river.

"What a great day!" Lisa cried, throwing herself onto the ground. Beneath the tree there were loads of red apples. Shanon and Amy picked some up.

"Yeah!" said Amy. "This day is definitely greenish."

"Right," said Palmer, "like the color of pond scum."

"How can you say that?" laughed Lisa. "Look at that river!"

The river below glistened in the sun like green glass.

The girls took out the letters from their pen pals. Each one had been read aloud over and over.

"I think Shanon's is definitely the best," said Lisa, rolling over onto her stomach.

"It's okay," Shanon said uncomfortably.

"Okay?" exclaimed Amy. "He called you a goddess! He liked your picture!"

"Well, I hope that's not all he likes," said Shanon. "What I mean is . . . looks aren't everything."

"Yes, they are," Palmer insisted. "That's why we've got to get pictures from *them*."

"We've already asked for some," said Lisa. "What else can we do?"

Palmer took an angry bite out of her apple. "Ask again. I don't know what you three are all so happy about. We asked for pictures and they deliberately didn't send any."

"It does seem strange that none of them even mentioned anything about pictures," Shanon said quietly.

"That's right!" Palmer jumped in. "Don't you realize what we're doing? We're writing to a bunch of guys who may look absolutely horrible! They may be the most disgusting-looking people in the world and we don't even know it!"

"Rob couldn't be disgusting," Lisa sighed, looking at her letter. "I can't believe all the neat things he's done. He's almost a hero."

"If you can believe him," Palmer muttered.

Lisa's eyes got bigger. "Why shouldn't I?"

"Why should you?" Palmer argued. "How can you tell if a person's honest if you can't see his face? And didn't he lie the first time about being a centerfold?"

"Hold on there," said Lisa, getting angry. "Don't you call my pen pal a liar! You're just jealous."

Palmer's face turned pink. "I am not!"

"I think you are," Amy said. "It's no secret that you still don't like John."

"Well, why should I?" snapped Palmer. "First he sends me that depressing poem, and now I find out he wants to get in shape so he can run away in case we have a war or something! I think his letter was really a downer."

"He said your picture was beautiful," Shanon reminded her.

"Well, that part was okay," Palmer said, somewhat

90

appeased. "But I still want to know what *he* looks like! If he doesn't want to send his picture, he must be hiding something!"

"I don't really need a picture of Simmie," Amy said. "Lisa's brother already told us he looks like an actor."

"So what?" Palmer said cuttingly. "He still can't spell!"

"He can so!" said Amy.

"He misspelled the word 'amusing' in both of his letters!"

"Anybody could have done that," insisted Amy. "And it wasn't 'amusing' he misspelled. It was 'amazing.' He said my letter was amazing and that my haircut was amazing."

"Amusing!" Palmer repeated.

"Simmie did not say my letter and my hair were amusing!" Amy said defiantly. "He couldn't have. That would mean he thinks I'm ridiculous!"

"Well, maybe he does," countered Palmer.

Tears of fury mounted in Amy's eyes.

"That's mean, Palmer," said Lisa. "Leave Amy alone."

"I wasn't being mean," Palmer whined. "And why is everybody always taking Amy's side? No one ever thinks about me!"

"Come on, you two!" Lisa laughed, rolling her eyes. "This pen pal thing is supposed to be fun. We shouldn't take it so seriously!"

Amy giggled. "Yeah, you're right. We're only writing letters to a bunch of boys."

Palmer cracked a smile. "And one of them is being tortured."

"That's better," Lisa said as everyone began laughing. "Our friendship's more important than the pen pals."

"Yeah," said Amy, "we're going to be living together for a whole year."

"Maybe longer," said Shanon, "if we stick together."

"I hope we do," said Lisa. "We make a great team." She looked at Palmer. "Don't you think so?"

Palmer flushed. "I guess so," she admitted. "I'm finally getting used to Amy's guitar-playing."

Lisa stood up and paced. "Now that that's settled, what are we going to do about this latest problem?"

"What problem?" asked Shanon.

"Palmer isn't happy with the pen pal situation," Lisa said generously. "If all of us are in this together, we've got to do something about that."

"What would you like us to do, Palmer?" asked Amy, trying to be fair. "Would you feel better if you had John's picture?"

"Yes," replied Palmer, sticking her chin out. "I have to be sure that he's not disgusting."

"Okay!" said Lisa. "We'll send the boys a formal letter asking for pictures again."

Dear Unknown,

We asked you to send your pictures and you didn't. We are willing to wait but would still like them. It is only fair since we sent you ours.

Sincerely,
Foxes

P.S. Please answer soon.

92

Dear Foxes,

We don't have any pictures to send you.

Signed,

The Unknown

P.S. Does this mean that you don't want to write to us?

Dear Unknown,

We have decided that we still want to write to you anyway. But since some of us don't know very much about you yet and you don't have pictures, we were wondering if you would mind filling out this list of questions. Remember that you asked us some questions the first time you wrote us.

Yours truly,

Foxes of the Third Dimension

P.S. Please send the letters to us individually. Thank you.

P.P.S. Here is the list of questions:

If you were a flower or plant, what would you be?

If you were a country, what would you be?

If you were a musical instrument, what would you be?

If you were an animal, what would you be?

If you were an ice-cream cone, what flavor would you be?

If you were a car, what car would you be?

If you were a book, what book would you be?

If you were a record, what record would you be?

If you were a color, what color would you be?

If you were an insect, what insect would you be? Would you be an insect at all?

Dear Lisa,

The other guys in the suite asked me to write you. The profs are really piling it on here so we cannot answer your questions, as the list is very long.

So long for now,
Rob Williams

The day Lisa got the letter from Rob, it was another "greenish" day, only this time all the Foxes agreed it was green as in pond scum.

"I feel sick," said Lisa glumly. "We may have just lost our pen pals."

CHAPTER ELEVEN

"This is it!" Lisa said, pointing at the bulletin board. "This is our chance!" Having just checked their mailboxes in Booth Hall, the girls were on their way to the snack bar. The only one with a letter was Lisa, and that was a note from her grandmother. There was still no word from The Unknown.

A large group of girls was buzzing around the bulletin board, where a colorful poster announced the annual Halloween Trickster Mixer.

"Do you think Ardsley will be invited?" Amy asked as the Foxes joined the crowd.

"Ardsley is definitely invited," a high-pitched voice replied. It was Dolores. "The only question is whether they'll decide to come. Last year's turnout was really poor."

"All the girls were just standing around," added Brenda, who was just behind her. "I remember—I was in third form then."

"Was the music rotten?" asked Amy.

"The social committee hired an excellent band," Dolores declared. "But word got out that the dance was boring. Maybe boys don't like to wear costumes. I had a wonderful time—but that's because my boyfriend came over."

"I've invited a boy this year," Brenda said cheerfully. "It won't be like last time for me."

"But it will for us," Lisa said glumly as she, Shanon, Palmer, and Amy continued down the hall to the snack bar. "That's just what Reggie told me about the dances here," she added. "The only ones who have any fun are the ones who set up dates beforehand. If you want to dance with a boy, you've got to invite him!"

"That counts us out," said Palmer. "We don't know anyone to invite."

"What are you talking about?" exclaimed Lisa. "We're probably the only girls in third form who *do* know some boys!"

Shanon felt her face pale. Lisa had to be talking about their pen pals. If Mars came to Alma he would see what she really looked like. He'd know she'd sent him a phony photo.

"You don't mean we should invite The Unknown?" Shanon said weakly.

"Of course we should!" Lisa replied. "That was our main reason for wanting pen pals in the first place."

As the group made its way through the crowd in the snack bar, Shanon noticed Kate sitting alone in the corner. But when Shanon caught her eye, Kate looked away.

All four ordered milkshakes, then headed for the center table where they always sat. The discussion continued.

"We have to invite Rob and the others," said Lisa. "This is a great opportunity. Just think—we'll be able to see The Unknown!"

"Aren't you forgetting something?" said Shanon, breaking into a sweat. "After they wrote that last letter, you said we'd definitely lost them as our pen pals."

96

"I know I did," said Lisa. "But this is our chance to get them back. When they meet us in person and—"

"Come to think of it," Palmer cut in, "it's not a bad idea. At least I'll be able to see what John Adams looks like."

Shanon's heart sank. Now even Palmer wanted to invite The Unknown to the mixer. She'd had a feeling that putting Doreen's picture into Mars's letter would catch up with her someday, but she hadn't expected it to happen so soon.

"What's wrong, Shanon?" said Lisa. "Don't you like your milkshake?"

Shanon stared at her untouched glass. "I shouldn't have ordered it. I shouldn't drink chocolate."

"I'll drink it," volunteered Amy, "if you're worried about breaking out. Do you want me to get you a vanilla shake?"

"Don't bother," Shanon mumbled, nudging the drink over to Amy. "I'm not hungry, anyway."

"Okay! Now all we have to do is figure out some costumes," Lisa went on excitedly.

Shanon nervously rapped her fingers on the table. "You heard Dolores—boys don't like costumes. That's why The Unknown probably won't come."

"Oh, I bet they'd come if we sent them a fantastic invitation," said Lisa.

"Anyway," Amy added, "Dolores said boys don't like to *wear* costumes. That doesn't mean they won't like costumes on us. You know She-Ra, that character on television?"

"Princess of Power?" said Lisa.

Amy nodded. "I've always thought she was kind of neat. I think I'll go to the mixer as She-Ra."

"She-Ra doesn't have black hair," Palmer objected. "If anybody should go as the Princess of Power, it should be me."

Lisa's mouth dropped open. "You don't seem like the She-Ra type, Palmer."

"Why not?" said Palmer defensively. "I've even got the costume—a little white leotard. All I need is one of those filmy short skirts and a cape."

"Don't forget your sword and shield," Amy said wryly.

"I get the feeling you don't think I could pull off a costume like that," Palmer said, her blue eyes flashing.

"I'm sure you could do anything you want to do," Lisa grumbled. "It's just that Amy had the idea first."

"No big deal," Amy said with a shrug. "Palmer's right. She-Ra does have blond hair. I'll go as somebody who's got black hair."

Shanon drummed her fingers nervously. All this talk about hair color was making her feel even worse, since it was one of the most obvious differences between her and Doreen.

"We'd better go," said Lisa, draining her glass. "Latin's in five minutes and I haven't even gone over the vocabulary."

"I've got a math test today," said Amy. She touched Shanon's arm. "Come on, we're going to be late for class."

"You go ahead," Shanon mumbled. "I'll be there."

Lisa, Palmer, and Amy hurried out, leaving Shanon alone at the table. Stealing a sip from the half-finished milkshake she'd given Amy, she rested her head on her elbow and groaned. "What am I going to do now?"

*   *   *

98

"*Amo, amas, amat, amatus.* I love, you love, he, she, or it loves—"

"*Amamus!*" corrected Shanon in a monotone. "It's not *tus,* it's *mus.*"

Lisa sighed. "*Tus, mus*—what difference does it make? The vocabulary test was this afternoon. It's too late."

"This isn't vocabulary," said Shanon. "It's grammar."

"Let's pack it in anyway," said Lisa. "Latin is a dead language. I prefer French. But right now I just want to write my letter to Rob—in English."

"Well, I'm studying my Latin," Shanon declared, burying her head in the textbook.

"Do what you like," said Lisa. "But we should all mail our invitations to the mixer on the same day." She crossed to the desk she shared with Shanon and pulled out some glue and colored paper. "I think I'll make an invitation," she said. "Something Halloweenish."

Shanon clenched her teeth and stared at her book even harder.

"Did you write your letters yet?" Palmer asked, coming into the room with Amy.

"Not yet," Lisa replied. "What are you listening to?" she asked Amy, who was wearing her Walkman.

"What?" Amy shouted.

Lisa stood up and got closer. "WHAT ARE YOU LISTENING TO?"

Amy threw her hands up. "I CAN'T HEAR YOU!"

"It might help if you asked her to take off the earphones," Palmer suggested. "Or maybe you'd better wait until the song is over."

Lisa nodded and took the letter Palmer was holding out to her. "You want me to read this?"

"I thought we ought to be in agreement on what we write to them," Palmer answered. "You could use my letter as a model."

Shanon glanced over her shoulder as Lisa read Palmer's note out loud.

Dear John,

We are having a Halloween mixer here. So I thought I'd write in case Ardsley did not get the notice. I'll be there too.

Hope to see you,
Palmer

"You're never going to get him to come that way," Lisa said critically.

"What do you mean?" said Palmer. "I think it's fine."

Amy took off her earphones and smiled.

"Welcome back," said Lisa. "What were you listening to?"

"The Grateful Dead," she replied.

Lisa pointed to the piece of paper sticking out of Amy's pocket. "Let's hear your letter."

Amy pulled the note out and read it out loud.

Dear Simmie,

I thought your letter was amazing too. And something more amazing is that we are having a big Halloween party here and everyone is wearing a costume. This party promises not to be boring. Hope you'll come.

Very truly yours,
Amy

"Not bad," Lisa pronounced. "But I don't think we should even mention the word *boring*. The mixer already has that reputation."

Palmer sat at the foot of Shanon's bed. "Where's your letter?"

Shanon put down her book. "I'm not writing one."

The other girls looked stunned. "Why not?" asked Lisa.

"Because—because I—I'm not inviting Mars," Shanon sputtered.

"But he'll come if you ask him," said Lisa. "I'm sure of it."

"Who cares if he does?" grumbled Shanon. "I don't want to go myself—I don't like costumes."

"That's okay," said Amy.

"Sure it is," said Palmer. "Just go as yourself."

"I can't go as myself," Shanon wailed. "Don't you understand? I can't go at all!"

"But you have to go!" cried Lisa. "Just think what you'll be missing if you don't!"

"And think about Mars," Amy added. "If the three of us invite the other Unknowns and you don't invite him, what will he think?"

Palmer nodded. "He'll think that Shanon thinks there's something wrong with him."

Shanon gulped. "I hadn't thought of that. Well, I'll write a letter explaining why I can't go. I can go home to visit my parents that weekend—anything!"

"If you're nervous about seeing him in person," Lisa said gently, "you don't have to worry. We'll all be at the mixer together."

"And if one of us doesn't like it," said Amy, "we can just leave."

"But it's not that I'm nervous," said Shanon. "Well, actually I am, but not for the reason you think." She got up and looked at her suitemates. "Oh, what's the use?" she said, her face red with embarrassment. "I might as well tell you."

"Tell us what?" Lisa asked, puzzled.

"I did the dumbest thing I've ever done in my life," confessed Shanon. "I didn't put my own picture in the letter I sent to Mars. I put that picture of Doreen in."

"What?!" exclaimed Lisa. "Why in the world did you do that?"

"Because of the pimple, that's why," replied Shanon. "How could I send him my own picture? It was awful!"

"So you just went ahead and put in your sister's?" cried Lisa. "Without even telling us?"

"Well, I don't blame her," Palmer chimed in. "I think using Doreen's picture was a good idea. After all, they do look similar, even though Doreen is a lot prettier."

"Shut up, Palmer," barked Lisa. "Aren't things bad enough?"

"It's okay," sighed Shanon. "I know Doreen is much prettier."

"But you have the same shaped face," Amy argued. "After all, you *are* sisters."

"But Doreen is blond," said Shanon, "and I've got brownish hair. And her eyes are blue and mine are hazel. So . . . you see why I can't invite Mars to the mixer. I just can't let him see the real me!"

Amy's dark eyes brightened. "Hey, we're forgetting something really important! This is a costume party— Mars never has to know what Shanon looks like, because she'll be in costume!"

"It'll have to be some weird costume to cover up my whole face," said Shanon.

"I've got it," Amy said suddenly. "It's a great costume and the perfect disguise. My mother made one for me in fourth grade and it was a hit. I even won a contest."

Shanon looked hopeful.

"What is it?" Lisa asked eagerly.

Amy grinned. "A refrigerator."

"A refrigerator!" Palmer screeched. "How can that be a costume?"

"It can," Amy said defiantly. "Mom made one for me out of a carton. You stand inside—you can even walk around. It's very comfortable."

"I'm trying to imagine what it would look like," said Lisa.

"You paint the carton white like a regular refrigerator," Amy explained. "And get inside of it. You can put a false back in it and even build shelves and glue on fake food and empty milk and juice cartons."

"Sounds complicated," Shanon said doubtfully. "Where does the person's head go?"

"Inside another smaller carton," Amy told her very seriously. "You can paint it to look like a big box of cereal."

Palmer rolled her eyes. "Original."

"It *is* original," Amy insisted. "Shanon will be completely disguised that way. There are peep holes in the head box so she'd be able to see, of course."

"It's beautiful," said Lisa, turning to Shanon. "Don't you get it? You'll be able to see Mars and talk to him, but he'll never know in a thousand years that you don't look exactly like Doreen."

"Right," Palmer muttered snidely. "All he'll remember is that she looked like a refrigerator."

Shanon felt sick, but she was tired of fighting. "Do you really think it'll work?" she asked weakly. "Suppose Mars asks me to dance, then what will I do?"

"Umm," said Amy thoughtfully. "We'll have to work on that one. Anyway, I could help you make the costume."

"And I'd be happy to decorate it," Lisa volunteered. "It'll be the most interesting thing at the mixer."

"Unforgettable," chimed in Palmer.

"Okay," Shanon sighed. "I guess it's worth a try."

Palmer got up and tore out of the room. "See you later. I've got to get started."

"Going to make your She-Ra shield?" Lisa called mischievously.

"No," Palmer called back. "I've got another idea for a costume. I don't know why I didn't think of it sooner. It's perfect!"

"Don't tell me you're going as a refrigerator, too, copy-cat?" Amy said.

Palmer stuck her head out of her room and smiled smugly. "Not on your life. I'm going as a princess—Princess Diana!"

CHAPTER TWELVE

Dear Rob, Simmie, Mars, and John:
Foxes of the Third Dimension
cordially invite you to the
Halloween Trickster Mixer at the
Alma Stephens School for Girls
Gymnasium.
BE THERE!!!!
Lisa, Amy, Shanon, and Palmer
RSVP
P.S. Wear a costume only if you want to.

CHAPTER THIRTEEN

There was only one light on in the single room, and through the half-open door Shanon could see Kate Majors bent over a book at her desk. It suddenly dawned on Shanon that Kate had probably never had a roommate. She was a real loner.

Kate turned at the sound of Shanon's soft knock. "What are you doing here?" she asked flatly.

"I forgot to give you the receipt from the printer," Shanon replied, pulling a crumpled piece of paper out of her skirt pocket.

Kate stared at her for a minute and got up. "Thanks." Ever since the day Kate had taken the pictures of the Foxes, they'd had very little to say to each other.

"I also want to apologize," Shanon added in a quiet voice. "I guess you think I should have told you that my, uh, sister—"

"Is Doreen Davis, the same Doreen Davis who went out with Bob Giraldi," Kate rattled off, finishing Shanon's sentence. "Yes, I think it would have been nice. Just when we were getting to be . . . friendly, I find out you're the sister of my worst enemy."

"Doreen's not your enemy," said Shanon. "She doesn't even see Bob anymore."

"Hmph," Kate muttered. "Well, that's one good thing.

Not that Bob even knows *I'm* alive anymore." She looked at Shanon suspiciously. "What did Doreen tell you about me?"

"Nothing," said Shanon in surprise. "She didn't even know you, did she?"

"Then how did you know I was the one who had a crush on Bob?" Kate quizzed her.

"I didn't—not until I saw his picture on your dresser. And only because Dolores—"

"Dolores was saying stuff about me again?" Kate cut in.

"She just said that you had had some kind of boy trouble," Shanon added quickly. "She wasn't being mean or anything."

"No, Dolores isn't mean," Kate said dully. "Not like some other people. She just likes to talk a lot."

Kate suddenly took a good look at Shanon, who was still standing uncomfortably in the doorway. "Is something wrong with you?" she asked. "You look sort of sick."

"I . . . I've got kind of a problem," Shanon faltered.

"Yeah, exams are coming up," Kate said. "The pressure can get to you."

"It doesn't have anything to do with schoolwork," Shanon said. "It's worse than that."

Kate crossed to her closet and got a white cardboard box off the shelf. "Want some taffy?" she offered.

"It's not chocolate, is it?" said Shanon.

"All flavors," Kate told her. "Sit down, why don't you?"

Shanon crossed into the room and perched on the edge of Kate's bed. Everything in Kate's room was so neat. Her brush and comb were set in a line on the dresser along with the snapshot of Bob Giraldi.

"Guess you're wondering why I still keep that picture,

huh?" said Kate, holding out the taffy box. Kate had made tight little balls out of all the old candy papers. Shanon took a green piece and slowly unwrapped it.

"Oh, is there a peppermint left?" asked Kate.

Shanon chewed. "So why *do* you keep the picture of Bob?" she finally asked.

"I don't know." Kate shrugged. "I guess I still like him in some way. It was the closest I ever got to a boyfriend. The Poodles thought it was hilarious."

"The Poodles?" said Shanon.

"One of the underground clubs here," Kate said. "It doesn't exist anymore."

"So there *were* underground sororities," said Shanon. "That's why you thought the Foxes were one."

Kate nodded. "Anyway, they thought it was a scream that a girl like me could have a crush on Bob Giraldi—or that he might like me back."

"He sent you his picture," said Shanon.

"He knew me before," Kate explained. "His mother and my mother are old friends. He was just being nice to me, but I thought . . . heck, who cares anyway?"

Shanon took another piece of taffy, this time an orange one. "So, these girls thought it was stupid for you to have a crush on Bob because you were younger than he was?"

Kate shrugged. "That and the fact that they thought I was a nerd."

Shanon blushed.

"Maybe I am a nerd," Kate said bitterly. "But that didn't give them the right—"

"I don't think you're a nerd," Shanon broke in. "I mean . . . if anybody's a nerd . . . I am."

"Don't be ridiculous," Kate said. "You're normal."

108

Shanon hung her head. "No, I'm not. I'm dumb, disgustingly dumb. I did something totally ridiculous." Tears welled up in her eyes.

"Hey," Kate said softly, coming over. "What happened?"

"I sent my pen pal Doreen's picture instead of my own," Shanon confessed miserably. "And now this boy is coming to the mixer to meet me."

"Gee," said Kate. "Why'd you do that?"

"Because Doreen is so good-looking," Shanon explained.

"But so are you," Kate protested.

Shanon got a tissue off Kate's nightstand and blew her nose. "Thanks," she said. "Anyway, I've decided that I will go to the mixer. Amy and Lisa are going to help me make this costume to disguise myself."

"Clever. What are you going as?"

"A refrigerator," Shanon mumbled.

Kate laughed. "What a neat idea."

"It's not a neat idea," said Shanon. "I'm going to look dumber than ever. And how will I be able to dance? I'll be wearing a huge carton!"

"That's tough," Kate said sympathetically. "Maybe you should just skip the whole thing."

"But I can't," Shanon said. "Lisa, Amy, and Palmer really want me to go. Besides, I sort of want to meet this boy . . . his name is Mars."

"Don't you think it's dumb to be going through all this suffering just because of a boy?" said Kate. "I mean, boys aren't everything. Look at me."

"You don't care about boys anymore?" Shanon asked softly.

"Oh, I care," Kate admitted, swallowing hard. "But I can't let the fact that I've never had a date rule my whole life."

Shanon's mouth dropped open. Kate was fifteen! "You've never been on a date?"

Kate's face flamed. "So what? If I really want to, I will someday. Like I said, boys aren't everything. Anyway," she added defiantly, "I'd rather spend my time working on the newspaper."

"I like working on the paper too," said Shanon.

Kate crossed to her desk. "I bet you're a good writer. Wish Dolores would give you a shot."

"So do I!" Shanon said fervently.

Leaning back in her chair, Kate put her feet up. "To tell the truth, I think *The Ledger* stinks this year. The stories are so boring."

"I think it would be nice to write about some current events in the outside world," Shanon added excitedly.

"I agree," said Kate, "like the fact that the Brighton River is getting polluted."

"Really?" said Shanon. "That's horrible. And it affects Alma and Ardsley, since we both use it for rowing."

"And it borders both schools," Kate added. She gave Shanon a smile. "I think we're on the same wavelength. The question is how do we convince Dolores? She's into reporting who wore what at which dance, along with every word Miss Pryn happens to utter. I think that's one reason why she wrote only a three-line article on the Foxes. She didn't want to even mention your being against single-sex education."

"Oh, we're not really against it," Shanon said quickly.

"We just think Alma's sort of old-fashioned. Not only in the social life, but in some of the courses, too."

"I agree," Kate said eagerly. "Quilting is nice as an extracurricular, but why don't they have woodworking?"

"Or auto mechanics?" Shanon added.

"And the career file is really outdated," Kate grumbled. "I'm going to graduate next year, so I've been checking it out. They're stuck back in the days when girls mostly became teachers or nurses."

"That's stupid," said Shanon. "Women can become anything. Lawyers, engineers—"

"Absolutely!" said Kate. "Even astronauts."

Shanon giggled shyly. "That's what I want to be."

Kate grinned. "No kidding. Well, it's been done before."

There was a moment of silence while the girls looked at each other. Shanon chewed her taffy and Kate twisted a candy wrapper.

"Why don't you go as one to the mixer?" Kate said.

"Go as one what?"

"An astronaut," Kate replied. "You could wear a helmet."

"Where am I going to get a space helmet?"

"Use a bicycle helmet," suggested Kate. "All you have to do is rig up a visor. The rest of the costume is easy."

"A helmet with a visor would cover my hair and face," said Shanon, brightening.

"And you could wear something really cool-looking on the bottom," Kate continued. "Borrow a jumpsuit from your roommate. You're always wearing her clothes anyway."

"Wow," Shanon murmured. "What a great idea! Thanks."

Kate shut the candy box. "Don't mention it. Want to take some candy for Lisa?"

"I already have a few extras," Shanon admitted. "See you later."

"Right," said Kate, getting to her feet. "Anyway, I'll talk to Dolores about some of our ideas for the newspaper. She owes me one for blabbing to you about my ... 'boy trouble.' " Kate shook her head and giggled. It was the first time Shanon had ever really seen her lighten up.

"See you around," Shanon said with a parting smile. "Thanks for the advice."

Kate turned back to her studies. "Anytime. See you at the newspaper office."

"Where were you?" Lisa whispered when Shanon came into the room. She was already in bed with her flashlight.

"Talking to Kate. How come you're in bed so early?"

"I'm beat," said Lisa. "And I think I'm sort of homesick."

"That's too bad," said Shanon sympathetically. "Maybe you should call your folks."

Lisa rolled over. "I'll call them tomorrow. Anyway, what were you doing with the enemy?"

"Kate's not the enemy," Shanon said, tossing her roommate some taffy.

"Kate's weird," Lisa insisted.

Shanon chewed her last piece of candy. "You'd be surprised," she said softly. "Kate's okay."

CHAPTER FOURTEEN

Dear Lisa, Amy, Palmer, and Shanon,
We are definitely coming to the mixer and are glad for the chance to meet you.

Yours truly,
The Unknown

P.S. Look for The Four Musketeers.

CHAPTER FIFTEEN

"Well, how do we look?" asked Lisa as the four girls lined up in front of the mirror. Only a few hours ago they'd been dressed in the regulation skirts and blouses. Now they were transformed! Tonight they were free to dress in a way that matched their wildest imaginings and to roam the whole Alma campus in that attire! It was Halloween—the night of the Trickster Mixer with Ardsley Academy.

"I think we look pretty cool," said Amy, flashing a smile. Head to toe in tight black leather, including a vest and jacket and shiny ankle-high boots, Amy was dressed as Joan Jett. Her glistening black hair was moussed to wild perfection, and her eyelids were laden with liner. On one wrist she wore a heavy metal bracelet.

Lisa had decided to come as a peasant. Her daring peasant blouse was pulled down over one shoulder, and her colorful patchwork skirt swirled at her ankles, just above her bare feet. Her arms were covered with friendship bracelets, and golden beads circled her neck. And in her long dark hair was a crimson silk flower that perfectly matched her deep red lipstick.

Palmer had decided to come as She-Ra after all, and was wearing a sleeveless white leotard and a short silky skirt made out of a scarf. She also had on a gold crown and a borrowed sword from the theater prop shop. The short, shimmering cape that Lisa had helped sew set off the costume, as did the stunning gold-dyed boots.

Shanon's costume was just as extraordinary; she didn't exactly look like an astronaut, but her outfit definitely had an other-worldly quality. She'd borrowed a silvery-blue body suit from Lisa and sewn fake NASA patches on each shoulder. On her feet she wore silver boots with the moon and planets painted in gold. The most important part of her disguise, a silver space helmet and visor trimmed with gold stars, was close at hand.

"Aren't we gorgeous?" exclaimed Palmer. "I think I make the perfect She-Ra."

"You do look great," Shanon said with a smile.

Lisa crossed to the window and looked outside. The gym was lit up so brightly she could see the lights even from Fox Hall. Girls from every dorm were crossing the quadrangle. "I guess we should be going," she said.

"Yeah," Shanon gulped. "It's time."

"That's right," said Amy. "We don't want the boys to get there before we do."

Shanon bit her silver-polished fingernails. "Maybe they won't come," she said in a shaky voice. "Maybe there's nothing to worry about."

"They will come," exclaimed Lisa. "But there's nothing to worry about anyway. All we have to do is look for some guys with feathers in their hats and then . . . have fun!"

"That's right," said Amy. "I just hope I'm wearing enough eye makeup."

The four Foxes looked at one another. "Oh, what's the use of pretending?" Lisa moaned. "I'm so nervous!"

"I seem to have a little case of stagefright myself," said Amy.

"What about me," Shanon lamented. "My knees are shaking. If this astronaut disguise doesn't work and Mars realizes I'm not—"

"Don't worry," Lisa encouraged. "It's all going to be fine. It's only a dance—remember?"

"That's right," Palmer said, surveying herself from every angle in the mirror. "We're going to be the best-looking girls in third form. The Unknown will faint when they see us."

Lisa eyed her. "I'm glad you're so confident."

Palmer gave her an arch smile. "Why shouldn't I be?"

"Let's go!" said Lisa. "No sense in putting it off any longer."

Shanon picked up her star-spangled silver helmet. "Just let me put this on," she said.

While Shanon tucked her light-brown hair under the helmet, Lisa, Palmer, and Amy put on their masks. They had decided to wear the kind that just cover the eyes.

"Are you going to take your coats?" Amy asked.

"Not me," said Palmer. "It wouldn't be She-Ra."

"But what about shoes?" Amy asked, seeing Lisa's bare feet.

"Peasants don't wear shoes," she called, skipping to the door.

Outside the sky was black and electric with autumn. A big yellow moon shone down on the four Foxes.

"It's freezing out here!" yelled Lisa as a gust of cold air blew by.

Amy picked up the pace. "Why don't we run for it?"

They raced across the chilly quadrangle, arriving in front of the crowded gymnasium, giddy and out of breath.

"Those must be the buses from Ardsley," Palmer said, panting.

Shanon lowered her visor.

"Don't forget!" Lisa said, leaning in close. "Whatever happens, at nine-thirty we'll meet by the punch table."

"I can't hear too well," Shanon said through the visor. "You have to talk louder!"

"Forget it!" Lisa shouted. "If you spot the boys, just go to the punch table! We'd better break up to look for them, though. There's a big crowd already."

"Look!" Amy whispered mischievously. "There's *Dan* and *Maggie!*"

The girls waved and Miss Grayson and Mr. Griffith waved back. Both of them were wearing plaid kilts and big tams. Lisa giggled. "Even in a skirt Mr. Griffith looks handsome."

As the Foxes pushed their way toward the entrance, Palmer stopped in one place as if she were stuck. "What is it?" said Amy. "Go ahead in."

"I'm going," Palmer said hesitantly.

"Don't tell me you're nervous too," jibed Amy.

"Well, maybe just a little bit," Palmer confessed. "After all, it's not easy to dump somebody. And that's just what I'll have to do if John Adams is disgusting."

They split up at the door and wedged through the crowd. Right away Lisa bumped into Brenda. Her blond hair was frizzier than ever and her face was made up like a cat. "Hi!" Brenda said cheerfully. "Is that you, Lisa?"

Lisa pulled up her face mask. "It's me, all right!"

"That blouse is too much!" Brenda said, smiling.

Stationed near the entrance, Shanon was jostled several times by the arriving revelers. The boys from Ardsley, especially, seemed to be totally unaware of who they were bumping as they elbowed their way through the crush.

Somebody knocked Shanon hard on the back. "Whew!" she heard a muffled voice groan. "This is worse than a rugby match." Shanon turned to see who was talking and almost screamed. It was a chicken head—or a boy dressed as a chicken in a three-piece suit and a T-shirt.

"Excuse me," he said, squeezing by her.

Shanon chuckled as she tried to make room for him. Who in the world would come to a dance as a chicken head?

"There you are!" Lisa was tugging at Shanon's sleeve. "Why are you still back here by the door?" She shouted above the music. "Have you seen them?"

"What?" Shanon yelled. "You have to talk louder!"

"HAVE YOU SEEN THEM?" asked Lisa.

Shanon shook her head.

"Let's go and find Amy and Palmer," Lisa said. She took Shanon's hand and steered her through the dancers. Amy and Palmer were already at the punch table.

"Any sign?" Lisa asked.

Amy shook her head. "No hats with feathers. The band is rad, though."

Palmer and Lisa got punch. "Want some?" Lisa asked Shanon.

"I'd better not," Shanon said through her visor. "I don't want to take this off."

"WHAT?" yelled Lisa.

"Never mind," Shanon mumbled. They'd only been at the mixer for a little while, and she was already uncomfortable. In order to keep her face covered, in case Mars came, she had to keep her visor down—which meant she could hardly hear or talk and couldn't eat or drink at all.

"Do I still have my lipstick on?" Palmer said to no one in particular. Her pink lipstick matched her face mask.

"You still have some," Lisa assured her.

"I saw the grossest thing," Amy said, stuffing a cookie into her mouth. "A guy dressed as a chicken head. He was very tall."

"I saw a short one," said Shanon.

"Maybe there are three of them roaming around," Palmer said, screwing her nose up. "Because I saw a chicken head too. Isn't that the most disgusting costume you've ever heard of."

"It sounds funny to me," laughed Lisa. "You'll have to point one of them out for me."

Suddenly the door burst open and a new group of boys entered the gymnasium. "It's some more guys from Ardsley," Palmer said excitedly. "Maybe the Musketeers!"

"There's my brother!" Lisa called hoarsely. "Hey, Reggie!"

A pencil-thin boy with dark shaggy hair waved from the door and made his way over to Lisa. He was wearing a blue blazer, gray flannels, and an eye patch.

"Hey, Reg!" Lisa said, giving her brother a hug.

"Hey, sis!" he cried. "I'd know you anywhere! Look at that blouse—whoo whoo!"

Amy, Palmer, and Shanon gathered around.

"This is my brother Reggie," Lisa said.

Reggie blushed and cleared his throat. "So, these are the Foxes."

Lisa's mouth dropped open. "How did you know?"

"Everyone in third form knows your real names. I heard some guys talking about you four."

"Don't tell Mom," Lisa begged. "She might not like it."

"She'd think it was funny," laughed Reggie.

"Lisa told us you didn't like the dances here," Amy said, offering Reggie a handshake.

"I don't." He shrugged. "Just thought I'd see Lisa. Anyway, this year there seems to be more action."

"What's your costume supposed to be?" Palmer asked, sidling over. "You're wearing an eye patch."

"Who knows?" Reggie said uncomfortably. "Captain Hook, maybe."

The band struck up a really loud number.

"Hey, Reg," Lisa shouted above the music. "Have you seen some guys dressed as The Four Musketeers?"

"Yeah," he yelled back. "They were on the same bus as—"

"Hi there, Foxes!" Dolores trilled, breaking into the group. Her gorgeous red hair was piled on top of her head and she was dressed as a flapper. "Isn't this a great turnout? I don't know what the Social Committee did different this year."

"Yeah, it's terrific," Amy complimented her. "You're on that committee, right?"

Dolores smiled. "I certainly am!"

"This is my brother," Lisa said quickly, keeping her eyes peeled for feathers. "Did you say you saw the Musketeers, Reggie?"

"It's nice to meet Lisa's brother," Dolores said, taking Reggie's arm. She peered at Shanon. "Is that you, Shanon?"

"It's me," Shanon mumbled, sweating under her helmet.

Dolores smiled. "Kate told me some of your thoughts on the newspaper. We should get together and—"

"Who's that girl dressed as a refrigerator?" Reggie interrupted, leaning in.

120

"Oh, that's Kate Majors!" Dolores announced.

"I'd like to meet her," Reggie mumbled. "A refrigerator, huh? Very interesting."

Dolores laughed and led the way. "Follow me."

"Where could The Unknowns be?" Lisa lamented, huddling with Palmer, Amy, and Shanon.

"Your brother did say he saw them!" said Palmer. "Maybe we ought to spread out again to look for them!"

"Look!" gasped Amy, as another wave of boys poured in. "I see feathers!"

"That's them, all right," Lisa breathed as four good-looking boys in plumed hats paused in the doorway. "It's the Musketeers."

"Look," Amy laughed. "There's another chicken head!"

"Who cares about chickens," said Palmer, smoothing her leotard. "We're about to meet The Unknown!"

"I'm going to faint," said Lisa. "What do we do now?"

"We have to go over there," said Palmer.

"I can't," said Lisa. "I'm going to die."

Cold sweat trickled down the neck of Shanon's space suit. "*You're* going to die," she moaned in a quaking voice. "What about me?"

"Let's go introduce ourselves," said Amy the minute there was a lull in the music and the dance floor began to clear. The four boys in plumed hats still stood near the door.

"Look!" said Palmer. "They're just standing there! They're probably looking for us!"

"That's right," said Amy. "They know what we look like."

"Good grief," said Lisa. "We've still got on these face masks. No wonder they haven't come over."

"Right. Let's uncover our faces so they can recognize us," said Palmer.

Shanon shook her head. "Not me."

"I didn't mean you," said Palmer. "You stay right under there."

The music began again and couples filled the floor. Lisa took a deep breath. "It's now or never."

"I wonder which one is John Adams," Palmer said.

"I wonder which one is Simmie," said Amy.

They started across the dance floor with Lisa leading the way, but the Musketeers didn't seem to notice them. "Why aren't they coming halfway to meet us?" Palmer said nervously.

"They probably haven't seen us yet," said Amy.

The boys stood as if rooted in place, while the four girls struggled to weave their way through the dancers.

Palmer looked over her shoulder. "Somebody's following us," she hissed. "One of the chicken heads."

Lisa looked back. "There are two of them behind us!" she chortled.

Amy looked back too. "Gross," she said. "And I think I see three of them."

The music stopped again and the Foxes were caught in the middle of the room, only a few steps away from the Musketeers.

"Hi," Lisa said, approaching timidly. Amy hung back with Shanon, while Palmer followed.

One of the Musketeers gave her a puzzled look. "Hi," he said in a low voice. "Do I know you?"

Lisa's face turned red. "I—I don't know," she stuttered.

"Of course you do," Palmer cut in.

Amy and Shanon crept closer. "What's happening?" asked Amy.

"I don't know," said Lisa. "They don't seem to . . . " Her voice trailed off as the girls were suddenly surrounded by chicken heads—now there were *four* of them! And they seemed to be waiting for something.

Suddenly Brenda came over to the group of Musketeers. "Hi, Lisa!" she said, grabbing the tallest boy's arm. "This is my boyfriend and his roommates!"

Lisa gulped. "Your boyfriend? You mean he's not Rob Williams?"

"Or John Adams?" said Palmer.

The tallest Musketeer chortled. "Nope, those guys are over there."

As Brenda and The Four Musketeers drifted away, Lisa and Palmer turned around—and found themselves staring right at the four chicken heads. Amy was looking at them with a bewildered grin on her face, while Shanon stood perfectly still as if she were petrified.

"Good grief!" said Palmer.

One of the chicken heads stepped up and tapped Lisa on the shoulder. "Hi, Lisa," he said. "I'm Rob Williams."

"Oh, no!" Lisa said. But then the boy took the head off and she melted. He was very tall and dark with thick curly hair and deep blue eyes—one of the handsomest boys she'd ever seen!

Lisa blushed. "Hi," she giggled awkwardly. "I thought you guys were coming as Musketeers."

Rob smiled. "That's what we thought too. But we had to change our plans. It's a long story."

Another chicken head stepped up to Amy. "Hi, Amy." He took the head off and a shock of thick blond hair fell over his forehead. He was very tan and had eyes that Amy thought were exactly the same color as Mr. Griffith's. "I'm Simmie Randolph the Third," the boy said, tossing his head back. "Your costume is very amusing."

Amy shook his hand and grinned. "Thanks."

The third chicken head stepped up to Palmer. "Hello there, Palmer," he said, revealing his own head. "I'm John Adams—your pen pal. I'm really pleased to meet you." He sounded very sure of himself, but the look in his light-brown eyes was warm and friendly.

"Hello," Palmer said, sizing him up. The boy had great red hair and muscles—not at all disgusting-looking.

"I like your costume," John told her. "She-Ra, right?"

Palmer smiled. "You got it."

The music started up again and Lisa, Amy, and Palmer moved off with their "dates." Shanon was left standing alone, facing the fourth boy.

"I guess you're Shanon," he said, taking off his chicken head. The boy was short with dark hair and fiery eyes.

"YEAH, I AM," Shanon yelled through her visor.

"I think I bumped into you earlier," he apologized. "I'm Mars. I didn't know who you were."

"RIGHT," Shanon shouted, trying to sound casual.

He reached for Shanon's hand. "Maybe we should get out of the way of the dancers," he said nervously. "This is worse than a rugby match."

They struggled across the room to the punch table. Shanon felt the warmth of his hand as he led her. It was a pleasant feeling. He filled up a punch cup. "Would you like a drink?"

Shanon shook her head and peered at her pen pal. He didn't look like a god exactly, but his face was definitely interesting.

He studied her costume for a moment and said, "Are

124

you going into outer space? Oh, that's right—being an astronaut is your secret ambition." He shuffled nervously. "I guess I never did tell you mine."

"WHAT?" said Shanon.

"I didn't get around to telling you about *my* dreams," he said loudly.

Shanon felt stupid. It was so hard to hear. If only she could take off her helmet.

"Why don't you take off your helmet?" he suggested.

Shanon froze.

"Take off your helmet," he repeated, passing her a cookie. "Have an Oreo."

"NO THANKS," Shanon yelled. "I'M NOT HUNGRY."

Popping the cookie into his own mouth, Mars looked down at the floor. "Listen," he said, "I think I'd better tell you something. . . . "

"WHAT?" Shanon shouted. "I CAN'T HEAR YOU!"

He looked at her. His eyes were friendly, but he seemed to be troubled. "If you'll take that thing off," he said, "maybe we can talk. I have something to tell you. Something I should have told you in the first place."

Shanon strained to hear.

He laughed. "Take off your helmet for a minute," he said loudly.

Her stomach turned over and over. Mars seemed like such a nice person. Shanon really wanted to get to know him or at least be polite. But with the helmet and visor, she couldn't carry on a conversation. Not only that, she suddenly thought, what about next time? Maybe there would be some other social occasion at Alma or Ardsley. The two of them would meet again. What would she do then? She couldn't keep her face covered forever. Oh well, she thought, here goes nothing. Slowly she lifted her visor.

"That's better," the boy said, smiling. "I can see your face, at least."

Shanon breathed a sigh of relief. He hadn't noticed her eye color was different from Doreen's.

"You know we were really impressed by that ad you put in the paper," Mars told her. "But when the other guys wanted to answer, I wasn't for it at first—"

"Wait a minute," said Shanon over the music. "I still can't hear you very well." She took the helmet all the way off. Suddenly, it was really important to stop pretending—to start being herself.

"Hey," Mars said, looking puzzled.

Shanon smiled. Her wavy brown hair tumbled to her shoulders. "I guess you're wondering who I am," she said shyly.

The boy's eyes snapped angrily. "You could say that. What is this—some kind of joke?"

"It's not a joke," explained Shanon. "You see . . . well, it's kind of hard to explain."

The boy looked around furiously. "Are my roommates in on this? Who's Shanon Davis?"

"I'm, er, I am," Shanon said, looking confused.

"You are not Shanon Davis," he said, pointing a finger. "You are not the girl in that picture!"

"No, you're right," Shanon mumbled, "I'm not. You see, I—"

"Great," Mars said sarcastically. "This is the Trickster Mixer, right? So, this must be some kind of a trick."

"But it isn't," said Shanon. "I *am* the person you think I am. I mean, I'm not, but I put in the picture and—"

126

The boy looked hurt and angry. "And had a good laugh?" he cut her off. "Well, ha ha! The joke's on me. I told those jerks I live with I didn't want anything to do with writing to any girls in the first place. And I was right! Good night!"

Shanon stood there with her mouth open as her angry pen pal turned on his heel and headed toward the exit. "But . . . I didn't mean . . . " she called after him in a shaking voice. "I mean . . . I'm sorry."

"And when you see the real Shanon Davis," he barked over his shoulder, "tell her that the joke worked, but it wasn't very funny."

The room seemed to swirl as Shanon stood there glued to one spot. She was filled with embarrassment and shame. Blinking back tears, she struggled through the dancers and ran back to her dorm.

When Lisa, Palmer, and Amy got home from the mixer, Shanon was already in bed buried under the covers.

"Shanon?" Lisa whispered. "Are you asleep?"

"Not yet," she answered softly.

Lisa sat down on the edge of her bed. "You sound like you've been crying."

Shanon sniffed. "Yeah."

"It really isn't as bad as you think," Lisa said earnestly.

"Did . . . did Mars say anything?" Shanon asked.

"No," Lisa admitted. "He sort of hid out until the bus went back to Ardsley. But Rob talked to him. He thought somebody was playing a trick on him. That there was somebody pretending to be you. But when he finds out that you *are* you—I mean that you're not Doreen's picture—everything should be okay."

Shanon sighed and rolled over. "I don't think so. It was really humiliating."

"It must have been," Lisa said softly. "But don't worry, it's not the end of the world."

"I know," said Shanon. "But I still feel pretty horrible—stupid and dumb and dishonest."

"Don't be so hard on yourself," said Lisa. "Any one of us would have put in a fake picture if we'd hated our own. What else could you do?"

Shanon sat up on her elbow. "I've been thinking about that. I didn't have to send a picture at all. Or I could have waited until my pimple had gone away and asked Kate to take another one. Anything would have been better than putting in a fake one."

"Yeah," Lisa said quietly, "I guess so. But you had no way of knowing that Mars would take it so seriously. Anyway, go to sleep now. Try to forget it."

"I'll try."

"Good night," Lisa said, turning out the light.

"It really is a shame," Shanon sighed quietly. "With a name like Mars, I half expected him to be weird. But he really looked . . . like someone I'd like to know."

CHAPTER SIXTEEN

Dear Amy,

I did not describe myself too well before, I guess. But I guess you have a good picture in your mind of what I look like after seeing me at the mixer. As for the rest, here goes— My name is Simmie Randolph III and I am named after my father. My hobbies are any sport, especially golf and tennis. I hope to go out for junior varsity. Interesting to hear you talk about soccer and music. I'm not much of a music freak, unfortionately. You'll have to teach me. (Ha-ha! Guess that will be hard to do by letter.) Anyway, signing off for now. I enjoyed meeting you at the mixer. I do like Joan Jet. You looked just like her.

Yours truly,
Simmie

P.S. What else should we write about? Can't wait until I see you again. You're a cool dancer.

"Isn't it great?" said Amy, strumming a loud chord on her guitar. She was sitting in her bedroom with Lisa and Palmer. While Amy idly plucked the guitar, the other two girls were eating grapes and bananas.

"It's nice," Palmer agreed. "Writing to Simmie will probably be lots of fun, even though he did misspell Joan Jett's name and the word 'unfortunately.' "

"Who cares about his spelling?" said Amy. "He's a great dancer."

"Yeah," Palmer said, casually popping a grape into her mouth. "I was watching the two of you dance. Simmie's awesome. When I was dancing with John Adams he kicked me in the ankle."

"But you have to admit John is really nice," Lisa prodded. "And handsome, too!"

Palmer blushed. "He does have good muscles, and the poem he sent me this time isn't all that bad, actually."

"It was beautiful!" Lisa gushed. "Read it again!"

Palmer unfolded her letter from John.

Dear Palmer,

I felt so great the evening of the mixer. It was wonderful meeting you at last. You were a fantastic She-Ra. Actually, you reminded me of a nymph in a myth or something. Have you ever thought of being an actress? Just want you to know also that some of the fourth-form guys I know were jealous that you were my date. I can't wait for the next chance to see you. But until then I hope we can keep writing.

Yours truly,
John

P.S. I am writing a poem in your honor. I hope you like it. This is the first line: "There is a run of mint in my garden holding back the falling leaves . . . its loveliness is only a mirror to you." I'm thinking of putting this to music.

130

"Nice," Amy said, hearing Palmer's letter for the fortieth time. "I wonder what kind of music he writes. Next time you write him, ask if he plays an instrument—okay?"

"I will," said Palmer. "It really is a pretty poem, isn't it? He probably thought of it after he saw me at the mixer. He said I was lovelier than mint."

"So you think you'll keep him as a pen pal?" Lisa asked with a smile.

"For the time being," Palmer replied brightly.

"This pen pal deal is working out so well for the three of us," said Amy. "Too bad about Shanon."

"Yeah, too bad," Palmer said. "Read your letter, Lisa," she directed.

Lisa's eyes lit up as she read the letter, and her voice was filled with excitement.

Dear Lisa,

Have you Foxes gotten over us chickens? (I hope not, because there's a lot of talk in our suite about you.) As I told you the night of the mixer, those chicken heads weren't supposed to be our costumes. But some fourth-form guys got dibs on those Musketeer costumes before we did. They come from the theater shop over here. You won't believe it, but we have plays at Ardsley without any girls to play the girls' parts. Dumb, huh? You know what I wish?—that the two schools could do some plays together. Then maybe we would both be in one together. Anyway, the chicken heads were the only things left in the costume shop that there were four of. Hope you weren't too grossed. You looked dynamite in that blouse and skirt you were wearing. What else can I say? Except, after I saw you

131

*that night I had this weird sensation. Like I had met you
before somewhere or as if you were somebody I'd known
for a long time. I don't usually feel that great with girls.
They have always kind of made me uncomfortable. But I
definitely felt comfortable with you. Also, when I and the
other guys in the suite answered your ad, we were sort of
doing it as a joke at first. But now I think it's a really good
idea. And I'm glad I've got you to write to.*

Rob

Lisa carefully folded the letter and put it back in the
envelope. "Isn't it neat?"

"Great," said Amy.

"It's a nice letter," Palmer admitted.

Suddenly, they heard the sitting-room door open.

"Anybody here?" Shanon's voice sang out.

Amy and Palmer hastily put away their letters. "We're in
here!" Lisa answered, stuffing hers into her pocket.

Shanon came in with her book bag slung over her
shoulder. Her face was flushed and her hair was pushed
back with an orange headband. "Hi, everybody," she said
cheerfully.

Amy, Lisa, and Palmer looked at her guiltily.

"Guess what?" said Shanon. "Dolores said I could write
an article for the newspaper."

"Wow!" said Lisa, jumping up. "That's fantastic! How
did it happen?"

"Congratulations," said Amy. "What are you going to
write about?"

"Maybe you could write an article about the Foxes,"
suggested Palmer. "And put in a picture!"

"You're close," said Shanon, taking a seat on the bed. "I'm writing an article about girls' schools. I've made up this survey and—"

"Survey?" Lisa broke in. "When did you do that?"

"I've been fiddling with it for a while," said Shanon. "Kate gave me some advice."

"Kate?" said Palmer. "What does she know?"

"Kate's been really nice," said Shanon. "She was the one who helped convince Dolores to let me write something."

"So what's the survey about?" asked Amy. "The social life at a girls' school?"

"Not only that," explained Shanon. "There are questions on the dress code and preferences for courses and extracurriculars, too. Then I'll compare it with what we have at Alma. There are some girls who might want to learn something like auto mechanics."

Palmer rolled her eyes. "Auto mechanics?"

Shanon laughed. "Well, I guess not everyone would be interested. But there are other things that aren't offered at Alma like—"

"How about the history of rock 'n' roll?" Amy said, getting excited.

"Or anthropology?" suggested Lisa. "We could go out on a real expedition and dig somewhere!"

"Not me," said Palmer. "I hate skeletons. But I would like to learn how to fence. Wearing that She-Ra sword gave me the idea."

"Well, you'll all get a chance to write these things down on the surveys I give you," Shanon said proudly.

"Where did you get the idea for a survey?" Lisa asked.

"From you," said Shanon. "Remember the questionnaires we sent The Unknowns?"

"Which they never answered!" said Palmer. "The next time I write John Adams, I'm going to tell him that."

Lisa shot Palmer a look.

"Sorry," said Palmer. "I forgot about Shanon losing her pen pal."

"It's okay," said Shanon. "I know you three have gotten letters."

"Palmer shouldn't have brought it up," said Amy. "We don't want to rub it in."

"It's all right," Shanon assured her. "Anyway," she added, "I got one too today."

The girls drew closer. "You got a letter?" Lisa exclaimed. "From who?"

"From Mars," Shanon replied quietly. "I guess it's the answer to the one I sent him."

"You sent Mars a letter?" said Amy, puzzled. "How come you didn't tell us?"

Shanon sighed. "It wasn't a regular pen pal letter. It was just something I had to do on my own. I had to explain that mix-up about Doreen's picture. I wanted to make sure Mars didn't think anybody was playing games with him."

Lisa gasped. "You didn't tell him about the pimple?"

Shanon smiled. "I didn't go that far. I just told him my own picture was terrible, so I decided to send my sister's— and that I was sorry about being dishonest. I figure that Mars and I are bound to run into each other again someday. I thought it would be better to set things straight now."

"That was brave of you," said Lisa.

"Well, why don't you read Mars's letter!" Palmer exclaimed. "I want to know what he said!"

"Okay," said Shanon. Her hands trembled as she opened

134

the small white envelope. "I didn't really expect him to answer," she mumbled. Mars's letter was written on green notebook paper and was folded several times. "It's a lot longer than any of his other letters," said Shanon.

"Read it," said Lisa.

Dear Shanon,

First of all, my name isn't Mars, it's Arthur Martinez. You probably think I'm conceited for giving myself a name like Mars—and that it was probably conceited to say I was a god. But I am not a conceited person. And I bet that you are not dishonest.

Your sister is very pretty, but so are you. And, to tell the truth, I was kind of scared when I got your sister's picture because she looked so sophisticated, and I couldn't understand how you could be in third form and look like that. And at least you did send something when I asked for a picture, which is more than I can say for myself. I didn't answer those questions, either (though the list is too long, I think).

So you see, you were braver than I was. I was really a chicken. Even at the mixer when I was about to tell you I'd lied about my name, I got scared. And then when I saw that you didn't look like the picture you'd sent, I just wanted to get out of there. Anyway, I apologize for blowing up. And if you don't think I'm too dishonest for not telling you my real name, then maybe we can keep on writing. I'd sure like to. From your letters you seem to be an interesting person.

Yours truly,
Arthur Martinez

135

P.S. It really was fun being called Mars like that. I kind of got used to it. You could still call me that if you like.
P.P.S. If I were a flower at all, it would be a stinkweed; and if I were a piece of music, I'd also be "The Star-Spangled Banner," only the way that guy in the sixties, Jimi Hendrix, played it. Sometimes that is the way I feel inside. Do you know what I mean?

"Wow!" said Lisa. "Incredible!"

Palmer giggled. "His name is Arthur?"

"I love the name Arthur," said Shanon excitedly.

"Are you going to write him back?" said Lisa.

Shanon smiled. "Of course!"

"Yaay!" said Amy. She strummed her guitar. "Now we all definitely have pen pals!"

"Yes, we've been very successful," Palmer said, giving herself a pat on the back. "We're probably the only girls in third form who have guaranteed dates."

"That's right," said Lisa. "We've all been on dates now—haven't we?"

"Maybe being in a group at a dance doesn't qualify," said Amy. They looked at Palmer.

"It certainly does!" she exclaimed. "Nobody's parents were with them! And the next time—"

Lisa gasped. "The next time! I wonder when it'll be? I can't wait to see Rob again!"

"I'd like to see Simmie again too," said Amy. "But until that happens at least we can write to them."

"Yes," said Palmer. "At last we know who they are and what they look like."

Shanon giggled. "At last we know The Unknown!"

"And this is only the beginning!" Lisa chimed in.

PEN PALS

Something to write home about . . .

five new Pen Pals stories!

In Book Two, Palmer thinks her pen pal John Adams is okay—more or less. But he's not nearly as smooth as Simmie Randolph the Third. Too bad Simmie already has a pen pal . . .

Here's a scene from Pen Pals #2: TOO CUTE FOR WORDS!

Mail call: Palmer watched nervously as Amy reached for the long cylindrical mailing tube with the Ardsley postmark. Of all the Foxes' pen pals, she was most jealous of Amy's. Palmer had only seen Simmie Randolph III once, but there wasn't a doubt in her mind that he was the cutest of the Unknowns.

Amy opened the top of the package and peered inside. "Looks like some kind of artwork," she said, pulling out the rolled-up paper.

"It's . . . a picture of . . . Simmie!"

"A giant blow-up," said Lisa, impressed. "It must be three feet by four feet!"

"Who cares how *big* it is," said Amy. "Look how *cute* he is!"

"Well we asked for photographs," breathed Palmer. She couldn't take her eyes off the poster. Simmie looked even better in the blow-up than he had in person. His thick blond hair fell over one eye and his eyes were a brilliant green.

"Do you think he wears green contacts?" Lisa asked.

"No, those are his real eyes," Palmer said dreamily.

"I think you're right," Amy agreed. "Where shall I hang him?" She walked into the bedroom and everyone followed.

"My side of the wall is pretty well covered," she observed. "I guess I'll take down Joan Jett."

"If it were Mars's picture," piped up Shanon, "I'd hang it right over my bed."

"Here's what we can do," Palmer said suddenly. She crossed to her own side of the bedroom. "My wall is completely empty—see? You can hang it here, Amy."

Amy looked doubtful. "Are you sure? Don't you want to hang something of your own there?"

"I can't seem to find the right thing," Palmer said, trying to sound casual. "I don't mind if you use it—really." She grabbed the poster and held it up over the wall space. "See! It's perfect."

Lisa nodded. "It is a good spot. If the moon is shining at night, his face will be lit up," she giggled slyly.

"That's right," Palmer urged. "He'll look great there."

Amy got the tape. "Okay. Let's hang it up. Thanks for letting me use your wall space, Palmer."

"No problem," Palmer said, pleased with herself.

Amy, Lisa, and Shanon went back to the sitting room, but Palmer stayed behind in the bedroom. Plopping down on the bed, she gazed up at Simmie Randolph III's blown-up portrait . . . and sighed.

Palmer's got a wicked gleam in her eye! But what's she going to do about it? What is Simmie going to do about it? And what about poor Amy?!

PEN PALS #3:   P.S. FORGET IT!

It's war between Palmer and Lisa! Palmer's pen pal Simmie Randolph III may be smooth and glamorous, but can she trust him? Palmer thinks she can, but Lisa doubts it—and tells her so. On the other hand, Lisa is sure that her own pen pal Rob is the most trustworthy boy in the world. Palmer sets out to prove Lisa wrong—and it isn't long before Lisa begins to wonder: If Rob is so great, why did he stand her up—*twice*? And why hasn't he been answering her letters lately? Is super-dependable Rob really a rat?

PEN PALS #4:   NO CREEPS NEED APPLY

Palmer is thrilled when she and Simmie are paired up for the first match in a round-robin tennis tournament. After they win, Simmie almost kisses her, and now Palmer's in heaven! But when Palmer starts to win without him, Simmie starts to snub her. To get back into his good graces, she desperately throws a match. Palmer then has to ask herself some tough questions—Is Simmie really the boy for her? Is any boy worth cheating for?

PEN PALS #5:   SAM THE SHAM

Palmer has a new pen pal. His name is Sam O'Leary, and he seems absolutely perfect! Palmer is walking on air. She can't think or talk about anything but Sam—even when she's supposed to be tutoring Gabby, a third-grader from town, as part of the school's community-service requirement. Palmer thinks it's a drag, until she realizes just how much she means to little Gabby. And just in time, too—she needs something to distract her from her own problems when it appears that there *is* no Sam O'Leary at Ardsley. But if that's the truth—who *has* been writing to Palmer?

PEN PALS #6:   AMY'S SONG

Amy and her pen pal John have written a song together, and it's great—too bad they can't agree on the lyrics. Amy finally gives in because she values John's friendship too much to risk losing it. Meanwhile, all the girls are buzzing about the class trip to London, but Amy is most excited of all. One of the Ardsley boys has arranged for her to sing the song in a London club. "Just don't forget my words," John warns Amy. But in all the excitement, that's exactly what she does. Will John ever forgive her?

P.S. These are just the first six books. There are more Pen Pals to come!